wake

Dispatches from Upstairs

Book One

sara ruch

DISCLAIMER

This book series is a work of fiction. Many gods and goddesses from different religions are mentioned. Some are based on historical and sacred texts, some are based on myths, and some are invented entirely in the author's head during long drives and sleepless nights. The author sometimes worries about things like being accused of insulting religions that are not her own. She assures you that she has nothing but reverence and appreciation for all the religions, stories, traditions, cultures and lifestyles throughout the history of both humans and gods on Earth and Upstairs. She thanks you for humoring her.

For Kriss
My first and most steadfast cheerleader

one

• • •

Chuli

I WOKE to the clang of a heater kicking on. Something was niggling at the back of my brain — something wasn't right. I was lying in bed. *Whose bed is this?* I opened my eyes, but couldn't see anything at all. I realized my wrists were bound, and that's when the panic set in. I tried to sit up, but stopped when someone gripped my upper arms from behind. My heart was racing, and I cried out, trying to break free from my captor.

"Please stop. I'm sorry about the blindfold and the hands. It was essential."

The effect of these words, whispered somewhere near my left ear, was immediate. My brain still flailed around my skull, desperately searching for moves from that self-defense class I took back in my freshman year of college, but for some reason, my traitorous body ceased all resistance. It was responding to the whisper as if the word stop was a direct command to be obeyed. It was terrifying.

"Don't be afraid. I don't want to restrain you, and I didn't want to drug you. It was the only way to save you. Please — let me explain."

With this next whispered proclamation, my brain

paused in its search for 'self-defense technique number 5', (was that the one that would break the opponent's nose?) to pay attention. The initial wave of terror receded — no, it was kind of metaphysically shoved down — and my whole mind-body package seemed to be signing on the dotted line, insisting that whatever was happening, the man that this voice belonged to was good, good, GOOD, and I needed more of it. I was no longer scared, but I sure as hell was confused.

I opened my mouth to say something. I wanted to show I was totally in control and that it's perfectly normal to calmly and rationally decide to let the man who'd apparently tied me up and put me to bed explain himself, because surely with a husky — *did I detect an accent? Oh Gods, I love accents* — whisper as thrilling as that, he could, in fact, have a perfectly reasonable explanation for all of this. Instead, when my lips parted, all that came out was a sort-of "mmm-guhh." *Did I just...whimper? Really?* I quickly shut my mouth again.

"Currently, you're innerly conflicted. Confusion and terror are being decimated by a rapidly strengthening feeling of desire for...physical companionship."

"What?" I struggled to understand, until I felt heat slowly uncoiling inside me. Oh.

I became very aware of the strong arms still holding me. My breath hitched, and I leaned backward, attempting to press against him. Instead of obliging, he let go of me and jumped up so fast that I fell backward, hitting my head off something. The wall maybe? "Ow!"

He leaned over and helped me scoot up and back so I was leaning against something solid, and apologized in another whisper, one I'd label contrite if asked. Why is he whispering, anyway?

As he helped me, I inhaled his scent. It was very subtle, and equal parts earthy and divine. He smelled delightful.

He backed away again, more slowly this time. *Nooo,* my body seemed to cry. *Come back!*

"Someone drugged you at the party this evening. It was urgent that I extract you, so I dosed you with a sedative to render you unconscious. It will clear out of your system quickly. I despise drugs, but in this situation, I believe it was the only way to stop phase 3."

He sounded resigned, maybe a little angry, but maintained his whisper evenly.

My mind spun. *Knocked me out because I was drugged?! With what? Who? How? What the hell is phase 3? And oh my gods, the PARTY!* I wasn't at any old keg party. I was at the posh New Year's Celebration at Boletto's, the hot new restaurant and club in the hotel just outside town.

I was dressed in an amazing little sequined dress I scored at the thrift shop a few months back, teamed up with my favorite pair of combat boots. I looked good, and I was stoked, because for the first time in freaking forever, I had a date. It wasn't just any date either. It was with the hottest guy around — Zach Hodson, expert at herbal lore and healing. Black hair, green eyes, and a wicked smirk, at least in his photos. Sharp wit and a great sense of humor, at least in text messages and emails. Sexy-as-hell accent, at least in his phone calls. After nearly two years, he was finally here, in America, on a book tour. Tonight was the night I was finally going to see the complete package, in the flesh.

We agreed to meet at the restaurant bar at 11:00pm, after he drove the 2 hours from the city and checked into his room. I had gotten my own hotel room too, so I could have a few drinks without worrying about driving home or having to spend the night in Zach's room if the date wasn't going so great. Last I could remember, I had come downstairs to the restaurant after unpacking. I was nervous, excited, and waiting for him to arrive, casually strolling around the party with an eye on the bar, saying hi to a few acquaintances I knew. *What the heck happened after that?* "Are we in my hotel room?"

"Yes. What did you drink last?"

My mind swerved course and tried to imagine what the person behind the whispering voice looked like. I pictured a big strong man with rugged good looks and sensuous lips. How would those lips feel brushing against my neck? "Mmmm," I bit my lip. *Man alive, I just moaned or groaned or something! Again! Get it together, woman! Fun-sucker, where are you?!*

A side note here: Most people have some kind of internal conscience, right? I've named mine 'Fun-sucker', because it has ALWAYS tried to keep me from doing anything fun or exciting. I usually found it annoying and had been known to do some stupid things just to spite it, but in this case, I thought it might be helpful for a change.

"It's difficult given the circumstances, but please try to stay focused. Do you remember someone giving you a drink?" The whisper seemed very kind and patient, as if knocking out and tying up women and questioning them was just a regular day at the office.

I thought back to the party. A nice waitress brought me a fancy cocktail. She said it was on the house. Maybe it's because I waited tables throughout college, or maybe it's because of the way I was raised, but I've always made sure to recognize and appreciate the efforts of others. I remembered thinking that we kind of looked alike. We both had long dark hair & hazel eyes with thick lashes. She had smiled sweetly as she offered me the drink. The cup — more of a chalice, really — was highly polished silver, with two intricately carved golden handles, and the liquid inside was my favorite color in the world. "Periwinkle!" I stammered out in the direction I thought the whisper was coming from.

"Pardon?"

The...drink ...was...periwinkle. The color. A waitress brought it. She looked like me."

My mouth was feeling exceptionally parched and sticky, but I was getting a little better at forming words together. "It tasted like a field in heaven. What kind of drug was in it? Ecstasy?" *Would that explain why I want to jump your bones even though you kidnapped me?* I left off the second part of that statement, because, well...awkward.

"It's something far more powerful than that. I suspect you won't believe the truth, for there are things in this world that humans have not willed themselves to see." He was still whispering. Apparently disappointment in the human race didn't warrant raising his voice.

Clearly this man didn't know me. If there was one human who was open to all truths, it was this girl right here. I, Chuli Davis, Little Brown Bird of Bear Mountain, spent my childhood with a dad who regaled me with wondrous origin tales of our Lenape ancestors, and a mom who tried on every religion like it was a new hairstyle, until she finally settled in as a Buddhist Monk in upstate New York. My dream job at Burning Wind Press — *Connecting Mind & Body to the Divine* — had me editing the works of a seemingly endless supply of authors with the oddest assortment of spiritual, devotional, and magickal knowledge. "Try me," I smirked.

He paused, took a deep breath, and then began. "The drug is an Amrit, made from the nectar of Veruni. I'll try to explain..."

This is where most non-Hindu people would be quite confused. But for me, Hindu stories have been especially near and dear to my heart since I was 12 and discovered a copy of The Mahabharata at the library. In fact, it's probably why I wound up with a double degree in Mythology & Literature. "I know about Veruni nectar. Balarama drank it and spent months consorting with Gopis in the Yamuna."

For some reason, this particular story resonated with me. I've always loved a good mythological debate, and I tend to ramble on when I'm nervous, so I continued. "The pompous douche broke the river into tributaries because he wanted to swim and screw in it. Who does that? Did he go back and apologize to Yamuna later, when he wasn't high? I sure hope he did. And what was he doing with all those Gopis hanging around, anyway? I thought that was his brother Krishna's deal. And where was his wife while all this was going on? Did she care, or was this par for the course when you're married to a god?" I paused for a response, although what did I expect the whisper to say? I had just kind of spewed out a whole lot of angry Hindu God trashing. Not exactly respectful or appropriate. I didn't even know who — or what — he was. Should I have expected him to know inner relationship details from an ancient Hindu myth and to have a nice little debate about it with a moaning drugged and bound chick?

I waited a few seconds, but there was still silence. "Sorry, I talk a lot. And I love Hindu tales."

The whisper finally spoke after a long pause, but this time it was barely audible. "Yes."

Ok then. I wiggled my wrists again. They were starting to hurt, but they were also feeling good in a fifty-shades sort of way. *Crap*. But I realized something. When I was talking, the drug managed to stay somewhat at bay. Now, in the returned silence, a wave of longing swept over me again.

He came closer, and I felt him sit on the edge of the bed. He leaned in close again, so close that his lips brushed against my ear, sending shockwaves of pleasure throughout me. "Do you feel the nectar churning in your insides? Do you feel it penetrating every pore, desperate for release?"

While he talked, he took his finger, and, starting at my cheek just below the blindfold, he slowly trailed it down my face. He stroked along my jaw. And with the gentlest of touches, he brushed his thumb against my lips. I cried out from the pleasure of it. I was on fire, and I liked it and feared it at the same time. "This is stage 2 of Veruni nectar. You think of nothing but release. Nothing but physical reaction. Each release begets another urge more powerful. The nectar grows in strength, until there is nothing left of you but pure physical longing for months."

Yes. Touch me again.

"Balarama was weak, and he succumbed."

I tried to think about Balarama again, but I couldn't form any more coherent thoughts. I nodded instead, and waited at attention for where his finger would arrive next, but it vanished. My body was now incinerating me from the inside out. I felt the sweat beads break out on my forehead, on the back of my neck — everywhere. I was covered in a sheen of perspiration that did nothing to cool me. I shifted uncomfortably until I felt him get up from the bed and heard him pacing.

"I've made it worse, and I apologize again. I was…I don't know what I was doing." He sounded confused, although it sure was hard to tell his emotions when everything was a whisper and I was feeling like a rutting pig. "Stage 2 is difficult, but you're strong. You can get through it. But you must not let stage 3 happen. It's irreversible."

"What happens then?" I managed to catch my breath enough to get some words out.

"Love. You will fall in love with the first person you make eye contact with 30 minutes after ingestion. If you're in darkness or alone, you will remain in stage 2 until sunrise."

I meditated on this for a second, trying to let the words sink in. I pictured them as cooling raindrops, slowly lowering my body temperature. It worked for a second, but then I pictured having wild sex in the pouring rain. Shit. Stop that! "In love?"

"Violently. Forcefully. You would be a slave. You would obey every command. You would live and die with the sole purpose of pleasing your beloved."

What a horrible way to live. Understanding dawned. "This is why you blindfolded me." If I could see him, I would be his love slave.

"Yes." He seemed relieved that I understood.

"Well, uh, thanks for that. I'm assuming the restraints are so I don't pull off the blindfold, but what's up with the whispering?" Could I fall in love with a voice without a visual to accompany it? Did I already fall in love with this voice? My body sure was acting like it.

"I didn't want to take any chances." He whispered.

We sat in silence again, but this time, I was ready for the next wave of longing. Now that I understood, I could almost make it out as a separate entity within my body. It coursed through me again, but I braced it with a deep yogic breath, like ducking under a crashing ocean wave. Not so bad. I just had to keep doing that for… "What time is it?" I asked.

"12:23."

Well happy freaking New Year to me. I sighed and waited for the next wave. This was going to be a long night.

---

two

. . .

Chuli

AH, *work, blessed work. Finally, life can get back to normal again. Is it weird that I hate vacations?* I wondered to myself as opened the glass door and strolled through the mini occult-like storefront to my office in the back. I got past the gargoyles, up to the healing crystals and was about to trudge up the small flight of stairs that led to the few offices of Burning Wind when I halted mid-step. There was a man in my office.

Through the big glass window that overlooked the store, I could see that instead of my lone desk, there were now two, nestled right next to each other. He was sitting at one, looking down. He had broad shoulders and man bun perched atop his head. I was completely alarmed for just a moment before I remembered. *The new IT guy!* How could I have forgotten?

In my defense, I spent a good chunk of my holiday drugged and then recovering. It took a solid two days of rest for my body to recover from the aches and pains and hangover-like nausea from the drugs, but my sense of trust and security in the world was a different story. It had crumbled completely to its foundation and was going to need to be rebuilt from scratch. In the meantime, I'd managed the emotional equivalent of pitching a canvas tent over the destruction and pasting a smile on my face until I could fully survey the damage and figure out who to call for help. I forgave myself for forgetting the IT guy. But even with everything that had happened over New Year's, one would think I'd have remembered an introduction like that! The dude straight-up passed out COLD.

Two weeks prior, I had been in my office, polishing off the last of the Winter Solstice cookies that had made their way to my desk. I had just turned on my vacation responder email setting when I heard Paul, my dear friend and boss, the owner of Burning Wind, talking to someone downstairs in the shop.

"Chuli, darling!" Paul called up to me, "I got you an early Solstice present!"

I came down the stairs, and, *Boom*! Before I could fully drink in the man standing with Paul, he collapsed in a heap, bringing down a shelf of rune necklaces with him. Instinctively, I ran over and kneeled before him. He was lying prone, with his eyes still closed. He was very pale, with black hair pulled back. He had thick eyelashes and full lips. *Da-yum. And he was for me?* I mentally chastised myself for admiring his looks when he could be hurt, except Funsucker seemed to dig him too. *What was up with her!?*

His eyes fluttered open and focused on me. They were a rich dark brown, with golden flecks near the pupils. He looked — alarmed? Scared?

We stayed like that, staring at each other, until Paul spoke, breaking whatever that moment was.

"Ram! Are you alright there, mate?" Paul seemed quite amused with the situation, but it was hard to upset him.

That was one of the qualities I loved most about him. To Paul, everything was entertaining, but in this instance, I was surprised he didn't seem at least a little bit concerned. What if the man had injured himself? What if he was sick, or dying? A chill ran through me, and I looked at him again. He had backed away from me, and was now sitting up and looking around. I watched the color return to his face, giving him a beautiful bronze sheen. As I stared, his expression became closed, serious, guarded. It instantly felt like a mask. *Huh.* He avoided looking at me. I figured he must be embarrassed.

"I...haven't eaten today." His voice was deep and rich, but clipped, as if he was angry.

I noticed a tourist couple gaping at us in the shop. We must've made quite a scene. The man sat on the floor, surrounded by runes. I was still crouched down, and Paul stood above us both, smiling.

Paul cleared his throat and offered his outstretched hand to help him to his feet. "Chuli, meet Ram. Ram is a computer...something, and he's here to help you build that dreamy new website you've been nattering on about for years now. He will start after vacation."

Ram ignored Paul's outstretched hand and got to his feet. Paul nonchalantly turned his hand to me. I didn't actually need it to stand up, but touching Paul always made me feel better. I'd sometimes joke that he was my own personal Blarney Stone, and I'd gladly kiss him for good luck, as long as Stewie didn't mind. He would joke back that he was older than stone and far luckier.

Paul put his arm around me. "Ram, meet Chuli. She is, without a doubt, the brains and the soul behind this whole operation. She will be your boss."

I gave Ram my brightest smile, and put my hand out in greeting. "So lovely to meet you, Ram! Welcome to the team! You may be the best present Paul's ever given me."

The last part probably wasn't true, especially considering the fierce look in his eye at the moment. The scowl he wore seemed awfully out of place for a guy who just got hired. He looked like he wanted to be anywhere but here, but he reluctantly shook my hand. Something surged in me when his hand enveloped mine. It made me want to cry out — *in fear? Relief*? But instead, I stoically smiled on as he dropped my hand and turned away. *Did he feel that too?*

"Well, I suppose I'll go take your new toy for a bite to eat. Apparently he's forgotten that mortal shells need sustenance. Stewie and I are heading into the city this afternoon and won't be back for at least a few weeks. Farewell, my Goddess. I'll miss you as always, and I'll see you upon my triumphant return." He swooped in and gave me a peck on the cheek. "I'll have Lucy sort those runes."

Paul and Ram walked out the door and vanished down the street.

With all that had happened to me over New Years, those two weeks seemed like a lifetime ago. As I stared up into my office, I remembered Ram's angry scowl. I'd been looking forward to getting back into the swing of things, focusing my energies on work to help me forget the New Year's Eve that had turned my formerly trusting world upside-down. But this new reality of sharing my sacred office space with a hostile man was turning my gut to stone, despite my enthusiasm for a new website. I really had been begging for one forever. The last one had been made in the Stone Age of the internet, when AOL and MSN were kings.

I thought of The Whisper, my imaginary superhero label for my kidnapper/savior. He'd given me very little to go by on what his own identity was — his true form was not human; and he was there to protect me and stop the person who drugged me. The Whisper told me I was strong. He was right. I would show this glowering hunk of man in MY office that I wasn't intimidated. I would march right in and kill him with kindness. It was the most disarming weapon I knew of.

Also, I felt kind-of bad that we had objectified him and treated him like he was something that could be given to someone else. Perhaps that was the reason he appeared resentful? I would've been! I squared my shoulders and attempted to harness my inner joy, ready to bounce into my office as if I hadn't a care in the world.

Just then, Lucy jumped around the corner. "Holy hot new guy!" She pounced on me and whispered by my ear.

I jumped and spun around, my heart hammering in my chest. "Jeeeeez Lucy! You trying to scare me to death?" *Is this my fate now? Frightened of everyone?*

Lucy laughed. As the only other female employee — in fact, the only other employee at all until Ram got hired — Lucy had determined that I was going to be her gossip gal. She loved to dish about everyone in town. She ran the retail shop at the front of the building, the one targeted to draw in the tourists, which meant she spent quite a bit of time socializing with the other shop owners and locals of the town. I wasn't a big fan of gossiping, but Lucy was the only other person I knew that was into Bollywood movies, so we forged a bond over that. Over the years, that bond had blossomed into true friendship.

Lucy continued undeterred, guiding me out of earshot of the office."I heard he fainted! I was out getting my coffee and only got a quick glance when him and Paul went into the pizza place, then I came back to this big mess of runes, and the customers told me a big man had fallen and taken them down with him! I cleaned them up, and the craziest thing....I swear the only ones lying face up were Wungo, you know, the one that looks like a P? but it was impossible to know if they were right side up, or inverted, so does he bring joy and comfort, or a raging frenzy? Either way, I finally met him today, and OMG he is so nice! Maybe those runes were a sign, Chuli, and maybe he is meant for me, my raging frenzy of comfort! His name is even Ram, like rom-com! I mean it's spelled differently, sure, but maybe we'll be stars in our own personal romantic comedy!" Lucy sighed and laughed at the same time, which combined into a noise startlingly similar to a maniacal laugh.

She looked at me, expecting a response. I had to think for a moment back to the thread of a question Lucy had buried within that caffeinated speech, a feat I was pretty good at after years of listening to her. She wanted to know if he had fainted.

"Yes, he fainted. He said he hadn't eaten."

I had a nagging feeling that it wasn't hunger. I thought back to the moment he fell. He seemed fine, looked up at me, went white as a sheet, and *boom*. Down he went. *Did he have some kind of epilepsy disorder?* I decided to Google it later.

As for Lucy determining he was made for her, I could see why she would think that. He was gorgeous and just the kind of man the two of us would ogle over if he were in a Bollywood film. I was glad of my no-dating-coworkers policy and even more glad Lucy knew it. There would be no weird tension or potential competition for his affections.

Also, this thing with Zach was still playing out, even though the date STILL never happened. I had managed to finally send him a text message to let him know I was OK around 2 am New Year's. I'd gotten adept enough at navigating the Veruni nectar that The Whisper untied my hands and hid in the bathroom so I could remove the blindfold and contact him. I told him I'd gotten a stomach bug or food poisoning. At The Whisper's request, I kept the details sparse, just in case Zach was the one who poisoned me, but why would he do that? I was clearly already willing enough. He wasn't Hindu, and his books never mentioned anything about Veruni or Amrits, only common herbal ingredients. Also, he was swimming with confidence and charm. I felt certain he would never resort to drugs to get what he wanted. *Or would he?* How much did I really know about him?

He was relieved that I was ok, and admitted that he had gotten stuck in a traffic jam trying to leave, and had to give up and turn around. He'd only gotten back to his home base in the city right before I texted him. I thought it was strange that he had never texted me to tell me he wasn't coming, but I tried not to worry too much. He was driving, so it was good that he wasn't texting and driving. Maybe he had planned on texting me when he got back, and I had just beaten him to it.

Plus, his story checked out. There was some kind of accident in the main tunnel that led out of the city, and the traffic was so bad it made the news. *Or was it some weird power play? OR...Maybe he was given the same drug, and he was afraid to say anything to me in case I was the one who poisoned him? Or maybe he was lying and wasn't stuck in traffic at all, just found it a convenient alibi, but didn't want me to feel bad for standing him up? OR...what if HE was The Whisper, texting me from the bathroom?!* I had agreed to attempt to meet up with him again when he returned from the first leg of his book tour in a few weeks. Maybe I could sort out all the mental confusion by then.

To complicate my dating life further, I couldn't help but feel a strong connection to The Whisper. Even though he kidnapped me, I understood why he had done it, and I just knew in my gut that it was a one-time thing. It was clear he was very upset with whomever it was that had given me the Veruni Nectar, and I felt comforted knowing he was looking out for me.

He promised to find the poisoner and whomever it was would pay. I wondered for the millionth time what he looked like. *Would I know him if he passed me on the street?* I knew he was strong, but had nothing else to go on, really. He urged me to be cautious and not accept food or drink from anyone. This made me a little paranoid and afraid, but given the circumstances, that was an OK way to feel right now.

Speaking of cautious and afraid, my thoughts turned back to my conversation with Lucy and the angry new guy in my office. *Did Lucy just say he was really nice? Weird!* Maybe I'd gotten the wrong impression of him. I finally brushed off Lucy with plans to get together later this week, and headed into my office.

"You're late," Ram glared at me while pointing to the clock on the wall.

"I'm sorry, I ran into Lucy and…" *Wait a minute! What am I DOING?* I stopped talking. *I was the one in charge here!* Why was I apologizing? I didn't do anything wrong. Burning Wind hours were always more of a suggestion than a requirement. I was the boss here, not this new guy!

I cleared my throat and tried for a voice of authority. "Let's get started. First of all, have you seen the old website? It's straight out of the early aughts. I've been compiling a list of changes I'd like to make, starting with a searchable index by genre." I put my bag down and sat down in my chair, inches from him. I could almost feel the tension rippling off of him. *Raging frenzy rune indeed. Nice? Comfort? Pfft.*

I turned my computer on. After what seemed an eternity of booting up, a box popped on the screen. "A critical security update is ready to install. It is strongly recommended for all users. Click here to install." The estimated installation time was 3 minutes. I could handle 3 minutes. As soon as I clicked OK, the wait time jumped to 45 minutes. *Great.*

I found myself more irritated by the minute. Ram insisted that before any website work was happening, we were going to the computer store to replace the "ancient rubble heap" I was using.

He had scoffed at my concerns about spending such an exorbitant amount of money without prior authorization from Paul, insisting that Paul had more than enough wealth to cover it, and that he would tell him that himself, which he promptly did in a text message.

A few seconds later, my phone had pinged. It was Paul, sending me a rolling eye GIF with "he's fun!" and then "have fun with your new toys!" and two more GIFs, one of a baboon shoving a computer off the desk in front of it, and another of a spoiled crying child stomping his foot.

I laughed out loud. Ram looked up with a questioning look on his face, but put his head back down again when I gave him a quelling "none of your business" stare. *Was he expecting a thank you?*

We headed out the door. I shrugged at a confused looking Lucy on the way out. Ram gave her a polite nod and smile, and she gave him a dreamy starry-eyed smile and fluttery eyelashes back. This brought my ire right back, effectively negating all the good happy vibes Paul's texts had given me. *Why was he smiling at Lucy? Did he think that's where women belonged, as simple cashiers, smiling prettily and blinking their mascara-ed eyelashes at customers instead of in power positions? What a prick.*

We walked to Ram's car, since mine was at my house, 6 blocks away. I liked walking to work, even on the coldest days, like today. The fresh air always invigorated me, and I liked the ability to stop and admire my favorite things on the walk — the tree that was beginning to eat the chain someone had fastened around it long ago and then abandoned, the old post that was probably used to tie horses to many years ago, and the way the sidewalk rose up from the roots of the trees pushing up. Even cement couldn't stop the growth.

Ram's car choice surprised me. It was a rather sad looking Buick from the late 1980s. I'd assumed he was quick to spend Paul's money because he himself had come from money too. And honestly, I'd figured he was rather vain, given his perfect man bun and crisp linen shirt. I kind of assumed he would have something a little showier, like some impractical 2-seater with fancy rims. I waited for Fun-sucker to scold me, as usual, for being petty and assuming, but it seemed she was still smarting over Lucy's flirtatiousness. *Was Fun-sucker jealous?* This was all too weird. She was supposed to be my moral compass and the foil to my spontaneous instincts, not a jealous Jane! *Was this how normal people felt inside? Shocked at the actions of their own consciousness?* I dared not ask anyone else, for fear that I'd be seen as even weirder.

People already thought I was weird. I wore mostly jeans and tee-shirts, never wore makeup, and I kept my hair in two braids 99% of the time. I grew up tinkering with motors and engines and other things that were typically the domain of men, at least in this rural Pennsylvania county. We may have only been a 2-hour drive from two major cities, but we were still years away from modern ideas like gender equality, gun control, and recycling.

A short drive later, and we were at the computer store. A salesman in a polo shirt greeted us. He had dark skin, dark eyes, and a pronounced accent. Ram asked him if we could view the desktop models that were currently in stock.

The salesman's eyes lit up, and he asked Ram a question, but it was in a language I didn't know. Apparently Ram did, for he answered him in whatever the language was.

The salesman looked elated, and launched into a long soliloquy. It seemed like the conversation was mostly one-sided, with Ram giving short answers here and there as they walked between desktop models. At one point, the salesman looked at me and then asked something. Ram shook his head. Then he said something else while laughing, and Ram got very still. The man seemed to shrink and pale as Ram said something very matter-of-factly to him. He then turned and went to the back room.

I was bewildered by the whole thing. "What language is that, and what did you just say to him?"

"Braj. He'll meet us at the register with everything you need. Let's go." and he started walking toward the register.

As I signed the credit card slip, I couldn't help but notice the salesman now seemed terrified. His hands were shaking and he wouldn't even look at me. He politely thanked me for my business, glanced another frightened look at Ram, and then slunk to the back room again. I looked over at Ram, who seemed very calm and confident and even pleased as he carried my new computer back to the car. He was definitely an arrogant asshole.

I was ready to burst with anger by the time Ram almost finished setting up my new computer. *The nerve of this guy!* He decided every single detail of my computer at the store, migrated all of my files and data from my old computer, and refused any of my offers to help. I was a do-it-yourselfer, damn it, not some sweet, mild, bride-to-be who let men make all choices for me! This was my new computer! One that I had secretly dreamed of having, but never worked up the courage to ask for, and would probably still be trying to work up the nerve if Ram hadn't intervened. But it was still mine! He wouldn't even be using it. He'd be using his own fancy laptop, so why should he get all the fun of setting it up?

To top it off, for some reason, he seemed so disgusted by me that he couldn't even look at me more than was absolutely necessary. I'd even peeked in a mirror to make sure I didn't have a booger hanging out of my nose, or food in my teeth. I was at the point where I was tempted to do something crazy, like rip open my shirt and yell, "If my face is so bad, maybe you'd like my tits better!" But honestly, I had very nice tits, and I didn't think I could bear the humiliation if he wouldn't look at them either, which he probably wouldn't. He'd probably just keep wearing that same stupid guarded look on his stupid guarded face with those stupid long eyelashes and stupid high cheekbones and stupid golden skin and stupid perfect man bun. Argh!

I stood up and stomped out the door, marched right past Lucy, who was helping a customer in the Egyptian section, stormed up the sidewalk, and didn't stop until I was home. I fumbled with my key, which was also infuriating. I had never had to lock my door before, but given the crazy circumstances, I needed to be on high alert, and The Whisper had told me it was important to keep my doors locked. I was even annoyed with him at the moment.

When I finally got inside, I grabbed one of my silk throw pillows, punched it, and then pushed it against my face while I screamed into it. I didn't want to alarm Mr. Richards and have him call the police. Just another man who would assume I was helpless. *Argh!* It was rare that I was in high dudgeon. What could make me feel better? *I know — dancing!* It was my favorite stress reliever. I went to my beloved vinyl collection, a hodgepodge of music compiled from my mom when she renounced all worldly possessions, my dad when he died, and myself over the years. Everything was better with music. I took off my sweater, boots, and socks, and gently placed the needle down on my favorite record, Orchestral Maneuvers In The Dark's *Crush*. Immediately, the beat began to make me feel better, just like it had since I was a kid.

I jumped and spun and gyrated. I shook my hair out of its braids, wild and loose. I felt the pure feminine energy of the Goddess elevate and heal me. All things that had happened today were trivial. I was above them. There was only the beat of the music, the beating of my heart, and...the beating at the door.

I stopped. Someone was definitely knocking on my door. It was probably Mr. Richards asking me to turn it down. Perhaps Mrs. Richards is napping? I ran over, turned it down, and whipped open the door while apologizing to Mr. Richards, but then stopped mid-sentence. It was not my landlord at all. It was Ram.

For a moment, we just stared at each other. He had a very strange look on his face. I was still feeling empowered from my dancing high, and I backed up, gesturing wide for him to enter. He hesitated, but then came in. He was holding my coat. I had been so mad, I forgot it at the office. I took it from him.

"Thanks. Forgot that. Did you need something?" I headed to my kitchen cabinet and grabbed a glass. I filled it from the faucet. I had forgotten to bring my water bottle to work. Between that and the dancing, I was feeling rather dehydrated. *Maybe that's why I'm cranky.*

I drank until the cup was empty, then refilled it, drank a few more sips, then sat it on the counter. When I looked up, Ram was still staring at me. "Sorry, did you want a drink too?" I went to get another cup from the cabinet, but he refused.

"Where did you go?"

"Home, obviously. How did you know where I live, anyway?"

"You left without saying anything. Why did you go home?"

I decided honesty was the best policy. "I was frustrated, and I wanted to dance."

He seemed very confused. "You...wanted to dance?"

"Yes. I like dancing." He still stood there taking it in. "You left work without saying anything? To go home and dance?"

"Yes, and I'll tell Paul myself. He has more than enough wealth to pay me to dance," I said, emphasizing with air quotes, mocking his earlier presumptive statement about Paul. I grabbed my phone from the counter and called Paul on speakerphone.

"My mysterious Goddess! How are things going with your boy toy and your new whiz-bang computer set-up?"

Ram seemed to flinch when Paul called him a boy toy. Interesting.

"Hi Paul! I'm good. I went home to dance. Ram is…" I was going to say he was a total pompous ass, but right now, he was looking around with an enraptured look on his face, as if my house were some kind of shrine. He wandered over to my alter and picked up the little golden Ganesha statue and stroked it gently. My heart softened just a little at that tiny motion, so instead, I said "Working very hard. Will you be in tomorrow?"

"You know I love your dance moves, my sweet little whirling dervish. I won't be back in the office until Monday. See you then, love. Bye!"

"Bye!" I hit the red button, then looked back at Ram. "Ok, well that's settled then. Thanks for checking on me, I guess?"

I strolled over to the record player, put the needle back on the cradle since the side had ended, then went to the door to give Ram the hint that it was time to go. He looked around one last time and then walked out, and closing the door behind himself without saying a word.

Why did he follow me? And how did he know where I lived? I recalled that I had just given him my address to register my computer. Still — I really didn't know anything about him. A chill swept up my back. He could be the druggist, for all I knew. He acted weird around me, that was for sure. And I'd just let him right in my house without a second thought. *Man, I suck at being guarded.* I was determined to do better in the future.

———

three

. . .

Ram

I SAT BACK on the sofa the High Order provided, feeling utterly flummoxed. For the first time I could remember on Earth, I had no idea what to do next. The assignment had seemed simple enough: Find whoever purchased the Veruni nectar, track them down, hand them to the High Order.

Once the assignment was complete, I'd planned to go back to my passion. I would utilize the High Order's network and pore over the Lost database, connecting the pieces like a puzzle until they clicked. I'd put in hold requests for any new entries, just in case they should perish before the documents were reviewed and the situation sorted out.

The database idea was still very new — 5 years old or so. I had created it myself when I was a teenager, as soon as my Knowledge returned. So far, I'd only been able to identify two Lost. I still hadn't heard what the end result was, and I wasn't sure if I ever would, at least in this life.

My earthly people-hunting and technology skills were excellent to have if one wanted to be an agent of the High Order, which is precisely why they had recruited me. I had agreed this time around, eager for the power and authority only available through them. In exchange, I had to agree to take on any assignments the High Order gave me.

I was still relatively new, so I'd only had a handful of cases, mostly drug busting. Desperate, bored, and sometimes sinister Forgottens often attempted to smuggle nectars and bloods and potions between the High World and Earth. I didn't mind busting slimy pieces of crap like that one bit. It was a job perk as far as I was concerned. Once identified, the suspects were then taken into custody and shipped back Upstairs, handed over to Those Who Judge. I didn't really know what happened and what kinds of punishments they were given, and I didn't care. I would finish a case, and then go straight back to my database work. Straight back to finding the one Lost that meant the most to me.

In this particular case, the nectar was tracked to a small town before it vanished. One of the Old Gods had reluctantly agreed to let me go undercover as an IT person in his company there, which seemed easy enough to pull off, since basically, that's what I already was. And now I was mired deep in it, for not only was I trying to build a complicated website from scratch, a skill just on my periphery, but I was doing it with her. *Chuli*, as she called herself.

I was so shocked when she strolled up to me, all smiles and confidence, that I actually fainted when I saw her. It was damn well embarrassing. She didn't seem Lost. But how would I know? This was the first time I had actually met or talked to a Lost, not just looked at their data on a form, and honestly, I had no idea what to say to her. She completely overwhelmed me. I would look at her, consider explaining everything, and then realize I had no idea how to begin, and turn away again.

It didn't help the situation that I had immediately started in on Paul when we left Burning Wind, accusing him of not following the new protocol and reporting her, when he had. In fact, Chuli had been one of the earliest entries. *How had she slipped past me?* I looked her up that very night:

> *Davis, Chuli*
> *DOB: October 30th, age 28 Earth Years*
> *Birthplace: Pennsylvania, United States.*
> *Father: Lenape/Native American*
> *Mother: Broadly Western European*
> *Former Name: Unknown*
> *Powers: Unknown*

She knew our world — at a place like Burning Wind, she was surrounded by Old Gods and Remembered and Forgotten all the time. Just about every damn book they published was by someone from Upstairs. But she was looking at it all with mortal, human eyes, right? *Did she remember anything? Did she know how to tap into her powers?*

There was a moment when I thought so, when she opened her door and power seemed to roll off her in waves, but I quickly deduced it was an unintentional side effect of dancing. Holy gods, she was beautiful in that moment, her hair wild and free, her skin dewy with perspiration. She had gotten supremely annoyed, apparently at me, and stormed home to dance. I had never heard of a god nor mortal that acted that way. Her little house, with her curated collection of sacred articles from so many different places, including the Ganesha statue, proved that she was full of love and adoration for everyone. It was humbling.

In contrast, I felt weak and selfish and boorish, which just made me more nervous, which probably made me appear rude, which annoyed her, which made me nervous and worrisome, which perpetuated itself as more rudeness, which annoyed her even more. It was a vicious cycle, and I didn't know how to break it.

I'd practically threatened to tear that poor boy at the computer store limb from limb for simply suggesting he could get her phone number. It felt good for a moment to be powerful and threatening, like in the good old days, when I could prowl around with my mace and plow, looking menacing. But the effect was short-lived. I went right back to being Ram the annoying IT guy.

---

four

. . .

Chuli

Dear Kunchen,

I hope this new year finds you well. I know that you can't write me back, though technically, written words aren't spoken, so they wouldn't break your vow, right? Things here are…

I PAUSED in my letter to Mom, or Kunchen as she wished to be called now. I wasn't really sure what else to write. I longed to tell her what happened, about how my trusting world had shattered. My mom was my best friend. She was the one person on the planet who truly understood me and could help me analyze anything that happened and help me determine my next moves, and she was hours away at a Buddhist Monastery, completely cut off from the world. My dad taught me the physical way of the world, how to fix and repair and understand the mechanics of things, but it was my Mom who helped me navigate the turbulent waters of relationships, personalities, and communication. I missed her fiercely, and I couldn't wait for her vow of silence to finally be lifted. I was pretty sure it was sometime soon, but I wasn't quite sure.

In the meantime, I diligently wrote to her, so at least she

would be completely in the loop of my life when she could speak again. Usually, the words flowed freely, but today, I could not seem to shape them, and I felt more alone than ever.

I put my pen down and decided some fresh air and company would do me some good this morning. I shoved my hands in my hot pink mittens and donned my yellow puffy coat and headed out the door to Paul & Stewie's house, a beautiful Victorian named The Chateau, just a few blocks up the hill. He and Stewie had come back from their apartment in NYC late last night.

I felt a little shameful coming over, especially so early. I really should give them some time to unpack, and I'd see Paul tomorrow at work, but I couldn't be alone with this burden anymore, and Paul and Stewie were my closest friends — my only friends besides Lucy, if I was being honest with myself.

As I walked, I considered this thought and how it came to be that way, especially since I still lived in the same county I grew up in. The beautiful Pennsylvania town I called home, nestled between steep forested mountains and a wide, clear river, drew many tourists from the city for day trips and outdoor activities. The more rural outlying areas surrounding the town, however, were still a little slow to progress, and mostly consisted of residents who had never been outside the state, let alone the country.

Even before I went away to college, I always felt like there was a whole world out there, and our region was just one tiny blip on the radar. The few friends I did have from my childhood had all moved away.

I'd strongly considered moving away forever myself. Going to the university in the city had exposed me to many different cultures, and I loved it. But fate had been kind to me, because not only had Paul been my absolute favorite professor, but as I was getting ready to graduate, he approached me with a job offer at the new publishing house he was starting, retiring from his University position. It just so happened to be right on my home turf. Paul claimed the town was love at first sight, and that he and Stewie were eager to have a quiet place in the boonies. And it meant I could be there to help care for my dad, who was sick and getting sicker.

5 years later, and here I was, approaching the door of the Chateau. After one quick rap, Stewie let me in. Gods, he was a pretty thing, with his porcelain skin and his big dark doe eyes. He looked as if someone had taken a statue of Adonis and wrapped it in a silk kimono and it had sprung to life. He and Paul had been married since at least before I met them, but he never seemed to show any signs of aging. He greeted me with a hug and a kiss on the cheek and offered me some coffee. I politely declined.

Stewie gave me a very long and poignant look. He then walked to the bottom of the stairs and called up. "Paul? Chuli's here, and something's...happened."

I stood there, shocked for a moment, but I shouldn't have been surprised that he knew something was eating me up inside. He was the most intuitive and observant person I knew. He gently guided me into the parlor to a comfortable seat, patted my hand and he promptly disappeared. He was excellent at intuition, but conversation, however, was not his forte.

A few moments later, Paul was there sitting next to me. As I looked at him, tears began flowing, and there was nothing I could do to stop the waterworks. I told him all about New Year's Eve: the spoiled date, the Veruni and the sedative I'd been given. As the owner of a mystical publishing company, I knew he would have no problem accepting the idea that I was telling the truth. I told him about The Whisper, but I left the embarrassing physical attraction parts unspoken.

For the first time in our acquaintance, he seemed...angry. Very angry. "Whoever did this to you will pay. Nobody fucks with my Goddess."

Angry Paul was a fascinating sight. It made him extremely intimidating. I was glad I was on his good side, and determined to never-ever-ever get on his bad side. I already felt a little better.

---

five

. . .

Chuli

FEBRUARY FINALLY ARRIVED, cold and bleak, which meant it was time for one of Paul and Stewie's legendary Valentine's Day celebrations to heat things up. Each year, their party featured a love-based theme with a focus towards getting wild and losing inhibitions. They were generally fueled by a tremendous amount of alcohol.

Usually, it was one of the highlights of winter for me. Given the circumstances, I was strongly considering skipping it this year, but Paul insisted that the safest place I could be was in his care. He reminded me that his party was invitation only, and the guests were highly vetted, and so here I was, nursing a fake cocktail in their kitchen.

6 weeks had gone by since my poisoning, and since then, there had been no sign of anyone attempting to do it again. I was beginning to wonder if it was just a freak thing. Was I just randomly chosen by someone for fun? But why would anyone have a drink of the gods anyway, especially in this small town? I didn't have any wealth or power. What would the benefit be? *It had to be random, right?*

As I mulled over these thoughts for the twenty-thousandth time, I tried my best to look like I was having fun, pasting one of those fake, closed-mouth smiles on my face as I stood in the kitchen. I was wearing a pair of red overalls with a pink tee-shirt and wore my hair in two cute buns on my head. I might have felt like a basket case inside, but at least I looked cute doing it.

As usual, the party was full of a fascinating mix of Paul's friends from the city. I knew several of them through work. This one over here wrote a book about tarot cards, that one about inventive ways to worship obscure goddesses. I was disappointed that Zach couldn't be here. I had been sure the New Year's debacle had ended things before they began, but within a few days, he began texting me regularly again, giving me updates from his book tour — funny little anecdotes, selfies with healers and people in our industry.

He sure was cute, with his green eyes and his short dark hair with a hint of wave. Sometimes he sent me pictures of gardens or buildings he thought I might like. They were usually not something that I would have picked out on my own, usually a bit on the more delicate, feminine side. But still, it was nice to have some kind of private connection to someone else. He even gave me a nickname: Big Bird, after the lovable Sesame Street character. Somehow it sounded really cute spoken in his British accent in the little videos he sent. He gave it to me because of my big yellow puffy winter coat, (yes, I sent him selfies back, too) and the fact that my name is Lenape for 'little brown bird'.

Someone taking such a personal interest in me was an especially soothing contrast to what I was experiencing at work. I just couldn't seem to make working with Ram pleasant. *Did the man ever enjoy himself?* I've never once seen him smile beside the tight, polite smile he gave to Lucy as he passed her on his way in and out of the office. At least Fun-sucker was no longer acting jealous. Lucy had regularly tried to engage him in conversation in the beginning, but her initial enthusiasm had worn off with each tight smile. Did I imagine that sweet look of reverence when he touched the Ganesha statue? I certainly never saw him that way again. If I had to describe him in three words, they would be *Scowling Man Bun*.

I tried to get him to talk about himself a few times, but the conversation always died. I was never one to blather on about myself to an uninterested party, so I didn't share anything about myself either. We mostly worked in awkward silence, and only ever discussed the website.

Sometimes, when I talked to an author on the phone, or chatted with someone down in the storefront, I'd swear I could feel him staring at me. It was a very uncomfortable feeling, as if he was looking deep inside me and I came up short somehow.

Although he had backed off somewhat, I still didn't care for the weird possessiveness he had shown when he first started, especially when he'd shown up at my door. In my head, it all lined up that he was the most obvious suspect. He showed up right around the same time as the Veruni, and was certainly not one to try casual dating.

Once, I had even tried to catch him off guard by asking him where he was for New Years. He looked suspiciously uncomfortable and said he stayed home. Paul had been in the room.

Afterward, he pulled me aside. "I know what you're doing. It wasn't him. Annoyingly arrogant, yes. Poisoner, no."

I trusted Paul's intuition, but still...something was not lining up here. He and Paul didn't even seem to like each other, so why on Earth did Paul hire him, and why had he not fired him? *And why was he defending him?*

He was, admittedly, doing a great job building the website. Perhaps that was why he was even more infuriating to be around. The man was really smart, and really talented. As I stood at the party and pondered all of this, I apparently took on a scowl of my own.

Paul was breezing through the room, and as he passed me, he kissed me on the cheek and said, "Kali, you're scaring the guests."

Kali was the Hindu Goddess of death and war. The thought that I could possibly resemble someone who went around with a necklace made of men's heads was enough to improve my disposition and make me laugh.

Then my thoughts wandered to all the gods and goddesses and mythical beasts and magical potions I had ever studied, and how the Veruni and The Whisper had been very concrete, physical proofs that all those stories could be true. Suddenly the thought that Kali could potentially be wandering the Earth was enough to make me shudder.

Stewie strolled into the room, dressed like Cupid, wearing nothing but a loincloth, carrying a beautiful woven basket lined with red silk, full of golden envelopes. The sheer beauty of him made everyone stop their chatter and stare at him in awe.

"Attention, please," he began in his crystalline voice. He used it so little that when he spoke, it always lent weight to his words. "It is now time for the party games to begin. All of you fine monogamous and asexual folks, please report to the parlor for a dance party. Everyone else, please take an envelope."

I thought a dance party sounded like just the thing to guarantee myself a good time, so I started to head out towards the parlor, when Stewie jutted an envelope in front of me. I gave him my best "do I have to?" pout, but he was unmoved.

I reluctantly took the envelope and stayed, awaiting instruction, while Fun-sucker seethed. That was all the determination I needed to know I was on the right path to my old, adventurous self, so I doubled-down and looked forward to hearing what kind of crazy game I was about to get involved in.

The game was called *Secret Assignation*. It was basically a glorified version of 7 Minutes in Heaven, the old party game where teenagers were closed in a dark closet together to make out.

Paul and Stewie had taken the second story and somehow created several private closet-like chambers, each accessed by one door on each side of the wall. On my card was written, "Red Bedroom, door 5."

Red and Blue bedroom folks were separated from each other as quickly as possible. The Reds went up the front staircase, and the Blues went up the servant's stairs off the kitchen, so there was little time to determine who possible partners might be. The other players and I were to take our places in front of our respected door. Whoever had the corresponding Blue Bedroom door would be my partner, and the only other person able to access our private chamber.

A large gong was to sound when it was time for me to enter the chamber, and a second gong would permit my partner. When the gong rang three times, all players were to exit their chambers and come back down the stairs to join the others for dancing. We could potentially never find out who our secret assignation partner was, or we could choose to identify ourselves and spend the remainder of the evening together.

I stood in front of my door as the lights to the Red Bedroom were turned out. My heart began pounding. *Could I trust enough to be fumbling in the dark with a stranger?* There was a safe word: *coyote*. Anyone could say that word and their partner would have to exit immediately and go downstairs, no questions asked. I reminded myself I was in a safe place, and I was having fun.

Clang!

The first gong rang out. I opened the door and stepped inside. It was a very small space. I was about to get very acquainted with whoever opened the other door. I placed my hand on the wall as I closed the door and noticed the soft padding lining the chamber. It was a luxurious silky fabric. This was a room designed for lovers.

Time slowed as I waited for the next gong. Cold, hard, reason began to creep in. I felt my heart hammer even more and felt the blood drain from my face. *Who was I to think I could just lose myself in a simple moment of bliss?* I turned around to face the direction of the other door and tried to steady my shaking hands.

Clang!

The second gong sounded. I thought I heard the sound of the door handle turning, but then it stopped. Several seconds went by. Did I hear someone groan? I was just about to turn around and flee when the door opened and quickly shut again in the dark.

"Chuli?" A low, concerned, familiar whisper said.

Wasn't the entire point of this game anonymity? So why did my partner already know my name? Then the familiarity of the whisper hit me. It was The Whisper! He was back!

"It's...you!" I was so relieved to have him here. After 6 weeks of radio silence, he was still around. I hadn't just hallucinated his existence in the first place. I wasn't crazy.

I wrapped my arms around him and held him tightly and tried not to cry in relief. *Damn, is he big and strong.* I seemed to fit against him perfectly. We stayed like that for several seconds. He was very tense, but tentatively held me anyway, finally slowly unwrapping my hands from his trunk, placing them in his own.

"I'm fine. I was just...nervous," I whispered. With the chambers all so close, I didn't want to risk us being overheard, but damn..was I ever actually going to hear more than a whisper out of The Whisper? *And what would I call him then?*

"You should be nervous. What the hell are you doing, playing this stupid, stupid game? Are you trying to make yourself as helpless as possible?"

I took a step slightly back from him, and my back immediately touched the soft padded wall. Apparently the wall was going to be the most comforting thing in the room. His tenseness began to make sense. He was apparently furious. With me.

I opened my mouth to respond, but he cut me off. "First of all, I saw you drinking cocktails earlier. I specifically told you NOT to take drinks from anyone. So first you start drinking, and now you just put yourself in a chamber for anyone to compromise? What the hell are you thinking? Do you have a death wish? How can I keep you safe if you're not even willing to keep yourself safe?"

Angry tears stung my eyes. *How dare he?* I pulled my hands from his. It proved difficult, because he was gripping them tighter the more he reprimanded me. I finally succeeded with a jerking movement and started back in on him.

"First of all," I began, mocking his earlier list, "I was NOT drinking cocktails! And how would you know? Were you spying on me? If you were spying on me properly, you would have noticed that I was secretly pouring my OWN seltzer water from home that I stashed in my purse into a fancy glass to fit in. People don't want to party with a sober person at something like this. It's a lot easier to just pretend you're drinking too. Second of all, I do NOT have a death wish. Paul and Stewie heavily vetted this guest list and promised me I was perfectly safe here."

I took a breath and continued, still whispering back, but with the anger growing in intensity inside me. "I played this stupid, stupid, game because I'm tired of this new, jaded version of myself. For just a few minutes, I wanted to forget the dangers of the world and go back to being my happy old self, not some wretch like, like...Scowling Man Bun."

"Like what?"

The fury seemed to be draining from him, but for me, it threatened to spill over into full-on anger sobs very soon if I didn't pull it together. "It's just a stupid nickname for this stupid guy I work with. He's never, ever happy, and has this vibe like the world is something he is just barely tolerating. I don't want to live like that."

"You think it's better to make out with strangers in closets?"

"Yes. No. I don't know. It was stupid, ok? I'm sorry." The tears of anger were now making fast friends with the loneliness and despair inside me. One managed to escape. I quickly wiped it away, silently cursing. I did NOT want to cry right now.

Shit, shit, shit. This was going all wrong. He stepped forward until our bodies were almost touching. He leaned closer to my ear and whispered, quieter and sweeter than before. "I should've known better. I was wrong. Please don't cry. Please..." His lips came even closer, until they gently brushed against my closed eyelids, kissing away the tears.

For a moment I stopped breathing. There had been several times over the course of New Year's where I had wished for this, but that had come from a different place in me — the place where the nectar lurked. This time it was different. It felt so good and right and comfortable.

He slowly and delicately kissed a trail down from my eyes to my cheek, but mostly just hovered, his lips barely touching me, his breath ragged. All of the pain and fury and despair seemed to vanish until I felt nothing but my body and his, every contact point between the two now hyper-sensitive. I was afraid to move, lest I break whatever this moment was. His lips got closer and closer to mine. When the corner of his finally brushed mine, it let loose a sea of passion inside me and I turned into it, and kissed him with everything I had. *Did I hear him moan?*

He kissed me right back, matching my passion, and our bodies collided into the wall. I longed to run my fingers through his hair (did he have hair?), down his chest, all over him, but somehow my arms were already pinned against the wall, above my head, held in place by one strong arm. His free hand plunged into my hair, undoing the buns, but I didn't care. He trailed kisses down my neck and back up again. He lightly nibbled on my ear. I moaned in pleasure. I didn't want this moment to end, ever. His lips were on mine again. This had very quickly escalated from something sweet into something much more carnal. He unlatched one of my overall straps, and slid his hand up my side, lifting my shirt in the process.

Clang!

The third gong rang out and we froze. There was the sound of shuffling and doors opening and closing around us, barely audible over our heaving breathing. He reluctantly let go, and we both stood facing each other in the dark.

"I..." he began, but then quickly turned, opened his door, and departed in the darkness.

I stood there in wonderment for a moment before I was able to turn and open the door. I felt like I was in a trance, and practically floated down the hall to the master bath. I wasn't ready to take on the crowd downstairs. No way.

Holy hell. I look positively...ravished! I thought as I gazed in the large mirror. My cheeks were flushed, my lips were kiss-swollen, and my hair was a tangle of two lopsided buns. My overalls half hung down, and my shirt was riding up. Maybe I should have felt embarrassed about what just happened, but I couldn't bring myself to feel anything but joy. Here was physical proof that I was not insane. *The Whisper was not in my head. Hallucinations didn't kiss like that.*

I felt drunk on power and lust. The ugly monster of reality was trying hard to intrude, but I was locking the door on all those questions of *what does it mean? And will you ever see him again? Will you ever see him at all?* I was keeping that stuff at bay until after I at least finished enjoying this one blessed night. I was also steadfastly determined to continue to ignore Fun-sucker's weird contradictory sad / satisfied feeling. Nope, nope, nope.

Tonight, I was going to embrace joy, dance my heart out, and let the chips fall where they may. I took out my buns and raked my fingers through my hair. It was wild and loose and felt entirely appropriate. I fixed my overall strap and re-adjusted my shirt. I closed my eyes and remembered just how they had gotten this way. I bit my lip. It still tasted like him — Earth meets divinity. I quickly opened my eyes and splashed cold water on my face. I was never going to make it downstairs if I kept thinking that way. I took my empty cup, chugged water from the tap, and headed down to dance.

The dance floor was a sea of happy, dancing people. I closed my eyes and poured all the joy and lust that was bursting out of me into my dance moves. I smiled and danced and sang along when I knew the words.

When I was ready for a break, I walked over to the periphery of the room. There seemed to be a few people staring at me. Some of them looked very confused, others fascinated. It was a super-weird feeling, and one I was unfortunately used to in Paul's friend group, though not usually on this level. His friends generally had this disconcerting ability to make me feel like I was both one of the club and also distinctly other at the same time. *Nope. I'm locking the door on that feeling too.*

A tall, brawny man walked up to me. He looked straight off the cover of a romance novel, with his golden, wavy shoulder-length hair, five o'clock shadow, and most definite six-pack hiding under his tight tee-shirt.

"Are you Paul's sister?" he asked with a heavy Nordic accent and confused smile on his face.

"Uh...no?"

"Oh, I'm sorry. You were dancing, and it made sense."

Huh? I stood there confused for a second before he continued.

"I'm Gustov of Valhalla. This is my first time down here in ages. Forgive me if I offend. I do not know the customs."

He seemed nice enough. "Hello Gustov of Valhalla. I am Chuli, the Little Brown Bird of Bear Mountain."

He bowed, making the whole thing feel very official. I smiled, remembering my dad. He used to call me that when I was little, and he would also bow, and I would feel just like a princess.

Gustov took my smile as encouragement. "Might I have this next dance, Miss Brown Bird?"

I laughed at such a formal gesture in the middle of such a raucous affair. Some areas of the room were beginning to resemble orgies, but here I was, practically being asked for my dance card, like it was the 1800s. Coincidentally, that was last year's Valentine theme, a masquerade ball. Now THAT was a good time.

Poor Gustov must've thought I was laughing at him. He put his head down and looked at the floor, ashamed.

"Gustov, you seem very nice, but as you said, you don't know the customs. I am laughing because this is not the kind of party with formal dance partners. I'm taking a break from dancing right now, but you may gladly accompany me. Why don't you tell me about Valhalla?"

He seemed relieved. "Oh, I see. Such a strange party. In Valhalla, it's just feats of strength and eating boar, and always, ALWAYS training for Ragnarok. Well, Gustov here was tired of this, and wanted to experience one of Paul's famous parties of Earthly Delights before the end finally comes. Tales of the debauchery at his parties has even reached the hall of many shields."

What was this guy about? This whole Valhalla thing was pretty hilarious and clever. *I'll play along. Why not?*

"Oh, I have heard of your many shields! But does the hall really contain 540 doors?"

His eyes lit up. He seemed thrilled that I knew of Valhalla enough to play this game. Of course I did! I had taken an entire college course on Nordic Mythology. Fascinating stuff.

"Oh yes, but it is not very confusing, because the doors are numbered. It is not so different from the doors upstairs here."

Oh, so he played Secret Assignation too, did he? He was a pleasant, good-looking fellow. I was sure whoever had him as a partner was probably pretty pleased. I wondered if they were experiencing after-effects like I was now. I closed my eyes and tamped down a feeling of lust as I remembered The Whisper's kisses on me. When I opened my eyes, Gustov was looking at me with what appeared to be a mix of lust and fear. *Shit. Could he read thoughts or something?*

"How was your, um, chamber?" I asked him.

"Well, I am still confused about the rules of the game. I went to Blue Room, Door 5 like my card said. But before I can even open the door and go in, the safe word was whispered to me. It did not seem fair to be exiled before I even got to play, but this is Paul's house, and I will be a noble guest and follow his rules, lest I shame my brothers in Valhalla."

It dawned on me just exactly how The Whisper got to me. Somehow, he must have found out where I was, and cheated his way into the chamber, leaving poor Gustov to retreat to the dance floor with those who wanted no part in mysterious trysts.

It also occurred to me that Paul and Stewie had deliberately matched me up with this cosplay Viking. There was no way they were just randomly handing out door numbers. They probably pored over the guests, moving them around like a guest list at a wedding to determine who would have chemistry. Gustov was hot, only in town for some fun, and he was funny with all his Valhalla speak, but he seemed a little too into this cosplay thing. Altogether he was a nice mix for one night of fun, but probably not anyone I would consider long-term.

While I was thinking all this, Gustov was rambling on and on about their beautiful goat. *Was he talking about milk now?* The mixture of the crowd, his accent, and my wandering thoughts had me unfortunately glazing over everything he said. I looked at him as he spoke. He did have a lovely lush mouth. *Would it have made me feel the way The Whisper's mouth had?* He certainly wouldn't have made me feel as upset and misunderstood as he had when he accused me of having a death wish. He was looking at me now, concerned. *Shit. Had he asked me a question?*

I wasn't sure if I should admit that I wasn't listening, or just pretend I knew what he was saying. *He had just been talking about milk. Maybe he was asking me if I liked it? That must be it.* I smiled and nodded my head and said yes, despite the fact that I was vegan. I did NOT want to get into an ethical discussion tonight. He smiled back, grabbed my hand, and pulled me back out onto the dance floor. *Oops. Not milk, then.*

We danced, but it was kind of awkward, like our moves did not sync no matter how hard I tried. Gustov was a terrible dancer. The torturous song ended, and a slow one took its place. We were kind of stuck in the middle of the floor, so the least awkward thing to do at this moment was to keep dancing.

I wrapped my arms around his neck, and he settled his hands on my waist like it was a 7th-grade dance. He seemed scared, like he had zero experience with a woman in his arms. Maybe his feats of strength, always training bit was pretty close to the truth of the matter.

I leaned toward him and went on tip-toes to whisper in his ear. "Relax Gustov, I won't bite."

He looked terrified of my nearness. He tried to act relaxed, but he was regarding me as if he had accidentally walked into a lion's den, and all he could do was wait with bated breath to see if the lioness who was circling him would pounce, or walk away.

I thought of The Whisper again, and again, my body reacted. I opened my eyes. Gustov's face was very close to mine. He looked like a deer in the headlights. I was pretty sure I could do whatever I wanted and he would be helpless to do anything about it.

I briefly considered kissing him, just for badness, but ultimately decided I didn't want to do anything that would diminish the taste of The Whisper on my lips. It would be like drinking orange juice after brushing my teeth. *Or following the most decadent dessert with grilled boar.*

I broke the spell and turned my face away from his. He let out a breath and started talking again. He was describing the feats of strength games. I tuned him out again as my face scanned the room. I noticed a couple on the far side of the room I hadn't seen before. It was Ram and Lucy! *When did they get here? Did they come together?*

The more I looked, the less likely that seemed. Lucy was turned towards Ram, animatedly telling him something. Ram was standing with his arms crossed, the usual scowl in place. Our eyes locked, and for just a second, dancing with Gustov made me feel...guilty. Weird.

Maybe it was just a coincidence, and I felt guilty only because the poor man was still talking to me, and I just couldn't bring myself to care one iota about what he was talking about, much like Ram clearly wasn't listening to anything Lucy said.

Lucy tried for a casual arm touch, and he actually flinched and turned to glare at her. For some reason, I found that hilarious. I knew one of his weaknesses now, and maybe I would use it against him to make him squirm in the office. Not a touchy-feely guy. A thought occurred to me. *Maybe I could rescue all four of us from each other?* As the song ended, I interrupted Gustov.

"There's someone I'd like you to meet!" I took his hand and pulled him from the dance floor to where Lucy and Ram stood.

Ram scowled at us the entire time we walked towards them, but it took Lucy until we were nearly next to them to notice.

"Greetings, friends!" I let go of Gustov's hand and smiled and waved as we reached them.

Ram scoffed, apparently bristled by my affectionate term for him. We most certainly were not friends.

"Oh! Chuli! Holy...WOW! You look different. What did you do, get a haircut? Did you get plumping lip gloss like that one I told you about they sell at the store in the mall with the..." Lucy cut herself off mid-sentence as she looked up and up as she took in Gustov's presence. He smiled at her, and she blushed.

"May I present Gustov of Valhalla. Gustov, this is Ram of…" I faltered as I realized I actually had no idea where he came from.

"Mathura." Ram finished my sentence, but now had his glare trained on Gustov.

Gustov put out his hand in greeting, but Ram continued to stand with his arms crossed. *Was he puffing out his chest?*

Ha! I rolled my eyes and wondered why I had wanted to save him from his miserable time with Lucy. *Because with Gustov trailing behind me and his constant rambling, I was going to pass out from boredom soon.* Apparently, I would rather be supremely annoyed by Scowling Man Bun than listen to any more Viking speak.

Mathura sounded familiar. I was positive it was in India, but I wasn't entirely certain I could remember where. I saved Gustov from any more awkwardness by lifting Lucy's hand and placing it in his.

"And who is this lovely Earth creature?" Gustov stated while looking at Lucy. She giggled.

"This lovely Earth creature is Lucy. She is a big fan of runes. Do you know anything about runes, Gustov?"

Gustov looked absolutely pleased and relieved to be holding Lucy's hand, as if she were a cute little kitten he could cuddle. "Oh, well, we did not invent runes in Valhalla, but in Asgard, I met some Meldorf tribesman who carved me my own set out of boar tusks. Boar tusks are a common material…"

I looked at Ram, who had a look of horror and fascination while taking in the two of them. He looked over at me and I made the walking sign with two of my fingers while saying with my brain, *Make haste! Flee while we can!*

Ram obeyed immediately and we popped through the nearest doorway into the kitchen. "You're welcome," I smiled and laughed at him when we safely retreated.

"She is like a motor that is always running. She never stops talking at me. It's...painful." Ram shuddered to even think about Lucy.

I was kind of amazed. Those were the most personal, non-work related words Ram had ever said to me, or to anyone, as far as I knew. *Maybe he was different outside of work?*

"Did you enjoy your dance with the Viking?" He was

still scowling, but, strangely enough, I really felt like he cared about my answer. It must be that weird possessive thing flaring up again.

I decided to tease him a bit. "Oh, Gustov is SO fascinating to talk to!" He continued to scowl. "For instance, did you know that there are 12 variations of goat milk depending on the variation of the goat's diet, and that there are 54 different ways to roast a boar?" I feigned enthusiasm.

Then, something amazing happened. Ram's impenetrable countenance broke. He lifted one corner of his mouth, and he laughed. Not loud, and not hard, just a soft, brief, chuckle, but the effect was incredible. It lit his whole face up like he was a radiant being made of light.

I was absolutely awestruck. Ram — the real Ram hiding behind the scowl — was absolutely beautiful. The air seemed to change around us and we stood there like that for a few seconds. He was staring right back, as if he was giving me permission to truly see him.

The spell was broken, however, when Paul came in and wrapped a protective arm around me. "Oh, hello there, Ram. Enjoying yourself at MY PARTY?"

A few people nearby quickly scattered. It was clear Paul was annoyed, and most folks wanted to steer clear of any trouble. Ram's mask was back in place. The two stood, staring each other down.

"Was he...not invited?" I asked, concerned, as I looked at Paul. If he could crash the party, maybe anyone could. *Was I really truly safe, even here?*

Paul wrapped his other arm around me, embracing me in comfort. "Of course he was invited, sweetheart. I told you, we have bouncers at every entrance. No one is getting in without an invitation."

I relaxed a little. "If he was invited, then why are you annoyed with him?"

I thought it was a perfectly logical question. I looked at

Ram again and his eyes seemed softer towards me, as if he was thanking me for defending him.

"Just because he was invited, it didn't mean I thought he would actually show up, let alone..."

"Actually," Ram cut him off, "I was just leaving." And with that, he turned around, set his fancy glass down next to the sink, and walked out the back door. *So Ram was drinking, eh?* Maybe he needed that liquid courage to break open his shell a little. I wondered what would have happened if he would have kept drinking, and if Paul wouldn't have scared him away.

"Gods, he is such an asshole." Paul stomped his foot to emphasize his words.

"Maybe," I replied, "But I think I would love to see what would happen if we got him really, really, drunk."

Paul laughed and laughed, like the idea was preposterous and hilarious. "Me too," he finally said, before leading me back out to the dance floor.

The dancing was finally through. Happy but exhausted, I was just about to head up to the third floor into the room Stewie had prepared for me when I noticed Barb heading in my direction. *Shit.*

"Chuli, oh Chuli! Wait, child!"

I cringed inwardly. I had worked with Barb while editing her book, *Discovering Past Lives*, and was convinced the woman had done more than her fair share of hallucinogens, beginning in the 1970s and possibly through today. She made me feel extremely uncomfortable. I tried my best to smile at her as she caught up, pretending I hadn't been deliberately avoiding her all evening.

"Have you been doing those exercises I told you about, my sweet? Any visions? You must be ready in time!"

She gripped my arm in a death grip and put her face mere inches away from mine. Barb cared not a whit for personal boundaries. She had convinced herself that I had some kind of tangled knot blocking my chakras, preventing me from connecting with what she referred to as my "Knowledge," and that something of epic proportion was coming once I made it to 30 years old. Something that involved the spirit of Atlantis and one becomes two or some other such insanity. She admitted that this far from the astral plane, she could not give further details, but she felt entitled to make me her prophetic pet project.

She had subjugated me to all kinds of rituals, from chanting *Ommmmmm* at me for 45 minutes straight to drawing Reiki symbols all over my back. I let her get away with it while I was directly working with her just to keep the peace, but since her book was published, I'd gone out of my way to avoid her.

"Um, well, to tell you the truth Barb, it's been SO busy at work, and I still have two years…"

My excuses seemed to fall on deaf ears. She peered at me hard. "Whatever you were doing upstairs earlier helped. Your kundalini was pulsing. It was quite active. That's a start! Kundalini is a powerful thing. Why didn't I think of this sooner? Do you know who your partner was? Perhaps an evening of sustained orgas…"

"OK Barb, well I don't know who it was, so we can just stop that thinking right there," I interrupted her as fast as I could. The thought of discussing my sex life with this woman was enough to tamp down any leftover lust I may have been experiencing. *Just…no.*

"Well then, if we can't find that person, perhaps we can seek out another for you. There were lots of potential mates at this party. Just stay away from that Indian I saw you talking to earlier."

Oh god. Barb too? Just how many people had been spying on

me at this party, anyway? I was about ready to hide myself away and never go out in public again.

And 'that Indian'? The way she said it seemed so derogatory. It irritated me supremely. This woman had basically culturally appropriated Ram's spiritual history, and now she was treating him like some kind of undesirable.

"Ram is my co-worker, and I'll talk to him whenever I'd like."

She caught my bristly tone and backed up a little. "I mean no harm, Chuli. It's just, I saw him early in the evening and got the chance to study him. His aura isn't right. It's all mired in inky blue, the color of death, guilt, and grief. I don't normally see that color in our kind. I mostly only see humans look like that when they've lost someone close to them, usually by suicide."

Our kind? Suicide? *Crazy freaking Barb.* I finally shook myself free and said goodnight, then turned and went up to my room as fast as I could, locking the door behind me.

---

six

. . .

Chuli

THE NEXT WEEK at work was a long one. I still hadn't quite recovered from the party and the fitful night's sleep that followed. Every time I would finally fall asleep, nightmare after nightmare would assault me, just like when I was little. The dreams were all fleeting: I could never quite grasp what they were about, other than after each one, I woke up feeling bereft, terrified, and lonely. Perhaps it was Barb and her suicide talk right before bed.

My sleep improved once I returned to my own bed, under my beloved dreamcatcher, the next night — or it would have, if I wasn't thinking so much about that kiss.

I pushed myself on such adventures to get out of my comfort zone to make sure I wasn't missing out on anything in life, but when it came down to it, I wasn't really one for physical relationships without emotion, which was basically what the tryst in the closet had been. On the other hand, I was also learning, thanks to Zach, that I wasn't big on emotional relationships without physical companionship either, so I was left feeling like my life was very unresolved.

Zach was still texting me sweet little things, but now,

instead of eagerly anticipating his visit next week as I should be, I just felt kind of bad for him. After all, it wasn't his fault I made out with a supernatural non-human in a closet and had subsequently been obsessed with that kiss ever since. And, if I were being honest with myself, if I had really truly thought there was more to our relationship, I would have definitely chosen not to play the game in the first place. The ugly truth, though, was that I hadn't thought of Zach at all when I was handed that envelope, and that was the most telling of all. I was at least going to meet him face-to-face before I broke things off with him.

Juggling all these emotions made this the longest, most easily distracted work week ever. I kept losing my train of thought, and I couldn't seem to concentrate on the website content at all. I kept secretly sneaking looks at Ram. He was far more interesting than the Meet the Authors web page. *Was Barb actually right about something? Was that scowl just a mask of someone in deep pain? If so, who had done this to him?*

I had always been crap at looking at people's auras, but I tried to see if I could see any kind of inky haze around him, as Barb had suggested.

"What?" He turned and stared back at me.

Busted. "I...uh…nothing." *Nice, Chuli. Smooth.*

"You keep staring at me. What do you want to know?" He actually seemed to be open to answering my questions.

Wild! But where should I begin? I didn't dare ask something as personal as losing a loved one to suicide. I briefly considered asking him why he insisted on wearing that ridiculous man-bun that made him look like a frat-boy douche, but that was more of an insult than a question.

"I was...trying to see what color your aura was." I figured what the hell. Why not just tell him the truth?

His eyes seemed to soften a bit. "Well? What color is it?" he turned his chair so his whole body was facing me, inviting me to view his entire body, unhindered by the desk.

This was the first time I was really, truly able to study him. As usual, he was wearing a loose tunic. He was a pretty large man, but the style made it difficult to determine his body type, what was fat and what was muscle. *Did he have a bit of a belly under there?* Same went for his legs, though I was pretty sure he had to have some powerful thighs to fill out his pants like that.

He had his hands folded together. His face looked very soft and clean-shaven. I could see no stubble at all. He must've been very good with a razor. His stance and his gaze reminded me of the many Hindu God paintings I'd seen in my life, but he was dressed much too plainly for that in his tan tunic and dark pants.

"I bet you would look really good rocking a bunch of bling." *Did I just say that out loud?* Oops. Lord was I tired.

I winced slightly, expecting a full-on glower at such an overture towards someone who seemed as attached to his manly portent as Ram. Instead, he surprised me by shrugging his shoulders nonchalantly.

"I used to enjoy wearing lots of jewelry. I guess I...just got out of the habit. It's easier this way," he referenced the one simple gold band on his finger.

I was surprised I hadn't noticed it before. *Is that a wedding ring?* I was just about to ask if he was married when he interrupted.

"Any luck with my aura yet?"

Oh! Right. I was getting distracted from my own distractions. I concentrated and tried hard, but nothing happened. "Nope." I blew out a puff of resigned air.

"Here, take my hand. Sometimes it's easier when you're making physical contact." He held out his hand to me.

Have I been wrong about him this whole time? Right now, I couldn't seem to see the apathetic, jaded, Scowling Man

Bun at all, and again, I questioned my own sanity. I just didn't know what to believe anymore.

I tentatively took his offered hand between my own. It was big and warm, and had calluses, as if he worked hard. Huh. I wouldn't expect that from an IT guy.

I stared at him again. I closed my eyes to focus my mind, and then opened them again. It seemed as if maybe the air was changing around him a little bit.

"I think it's working!" I exclaimed in wonderment as color particles seemed to be appearing in the air and joining together like some kind of colorful condensation. Just as I leaned in towards him for a closer look, my office door flew open.

"Chuli!" Paul's voice boomed into my office.

I guiltily dropped Ram's hand as if I had been caught doing something bad and tried not to think about how I had enjoyed its warmth quite a bit. I realized that through the window, it probably looked like we were having some kind of intimate moment. I supposed we were, but not in that way.

"Can I see you for a minute?" He smiled at me, but dropped all friendliness by the time his gaze reached Ram.

"Uh...sure," I stood up and walked out to follow Paul. He took me into his office and closed the door.

"Don't get involved with him, Chuli."

I went to protest, but he held up his hand and continued," I know what you're going to say, you just want to help him, there's no harm in being nice, blah blah blah. You always want to see the best in people and help them, but I'm telling you, Chuli, do not trust him. Do not get involved. It will only get you hurt in the end."

"I...how…" I began, but I was so flustered by what he was saying that I didn't even know how to respond.

Paul had always been easy and carefree, and while I knew he had my back, he had never once given me a direct order to stay away from someone, let alone a fellow co-worker.

"Why is he here then, if he is so untrustworthy?" I spat out, finally finding words.

"He will be gone as soon as the website is finished. So please just do everything in your power to make that happen as fast as possible and Do. Not. Get. Involved. With. Him." He opened his office door and stormed out, ranting under his breath, mumbling something about a high order, and sanctimonious bastards. *This was too weird.*

On my way out of the office, I glanced at Lucy. She had a prime view of both our offices and she raised her eyes at me in a "oh we are so going to talk about whatever just happened later" way.

I gave her my best "it's nothing" shrug back and mentally braced myself for whatever questions she was planning to throw my way.

By Friday afternoon, I had done my best all week to listen to Paul and keep the focus on work, and I was diligently finishing up a section on the website. At this pace, we were scheduled to complete the site within the next two weeks. I was the last one to leave the offices. Ram had left about 30 minutes before, and Paul always left by noon on a Friday. It was a slow time of year for tourists, so Lucy had already closed up shop too. I shut down my beautiful new computer, packed up my things, donned my puffy coat and left, locking the jingling door behind me.

On my walk up the sidewalk, I noticed Ram's beat-up old car. He was standing next to it. He looked cold and he looked pissed. *Do not engage,* I said to myself. *Remember Paul's warning.*

I nearly kept walking, but could it hurt to ask what he was doing? I stopped. "Whatcha up to, Ram?"

"The stupid car won't go." He sounded like a mad 5-year-old with a broken toy.

"Ok, why don't I take a look?" What harm could there be in helping to get his car started? I would've done the same for any stranger. Besides, it had been ages since I played under the hood of a car, the way I always used to back in Dad's shop.

I popped the hood and could almost hear my dad's kind voice behind me, guiding me. "Try to start it."

Ram climbed in the front seat and obeyed. It fired right up, but the minute he took his foot off the pedal, it stalled again. There wouldn't be much peering under the hood today. I knew exactly what was wrong, and it was more than could be fixed on the street.

"You'll need to have it tow…" but before I could finish saying the words, like magic, the tow truck appeared. A familiar logo was printed on the side. *Please be one of the guys...anyone but him,* I prayed to myself, but unfortunately, Tolly came hustling over.

"What seems to be the problem?" He was using his smooth as silk customer-hustling voice.

My back was turned, so he hadn't seen me yet. I braced myself and turned around. "Idle air control valve. Everything else is FINE." I emphasized the last word.

I watched Tolly's face turn hostile as he took in who he was talking to. We stood there for a moment, an icy showdown. "I'll tell John that too. I won't have you ripping him off, Tolly." I took on a very threatening tone, the one reserved just for him.

"You do that, Chuli. Why the fuck did you call me if you know all the answers?" He emphasized my name in that awful, accusatory way he always had.

"She didn't. I did." We both looked at Ram, who was

standing on the sidewalk. For once, I was glad for his intimidating glower.

Tolly sighed. "Well, let's get this over with." Turning away from both of us, he began maneuvering the truck and attaching the tow chains to the car.

I stood there, too tense to do anything but watch. I'm not sure what Ram was doing, as I was too busy trying to keep my breathing steady and to look unaffected by Tolly's presence.

When he was done, he deliberately ignored me. He looked at Ram and said, "Call the shop on Monday." And without offering Ram a ride, he hopped back in the truck and drove away.

For a moment, we both just stood in front of the empty spot that used to contain Ram's car. It dawned on me that I had no idea how far Ram lived, but it probably wasn't close enough to walk if he drove to work every day. *In for a penny, out for a pound.*

"We'll go get my car." He nodded in acknowledgment, and we quickly trudged up the street the 6 blocks to my house. I unlocked the door, dumped my work bag inside, grabbed my car keys, and headed right back out again.

Ram gave me directions to his place a few minutes outside of town. While I drove, I could feel his questioning gaze, and I decided to oblige.

"That, Ram, was my brother, Tolly. We have a...complicated history." If that's what you call a lifetime of abuse.

Tolly was 8 years my senior. As long as I could remember, he was kind and friendly and smooth as silk in public. But the moment we were left alone, he was a terror. He would call me horrible names and tell me the best thing I could do for anyone was to just die. He would even sometimes physically hurt me, but always in places where it was hidden. He would tell me that I better not tell on him, but even if I did, no one would believe a loser like me.

It got so bad, I started carrying a pen-knife with me. The last time he attacked, I defended myself. He still had the scar on his forearm. I left for college shortly after, so I managed to successfully avoid him for a long time. By the time dad got sick and I came to help him, Tolly had moved into a place of his own and was working at the busy shop nearly all the time, so it was easy enough to avoid him.

At our dad's funeral, he pulled me aside one last time. He painfully gripped my upper arm, and said, "Now the game is up. I don't have to pretend you're my sister for a second longer. Stay out of my sight, you little bitch."

Any onlookers would have thought he was offering some words of comfort to his little sister. If only they knew the truth.

That was two years ago. Today was the first I'd seen him since. Seeing him brought all that trauma right back up again.

"Boy, it sure is cold out." I tried to play off my hands shaking on the steering wheel as a symptom of the cold day.

I was pretty sure Ram wasn't fooled, but he said nothing. Finally, we reached his driveway. His house was small, but beautiful. It was tucked back in the woods, with some kind of greenhouse attached to it. *Ram, a gardener? Huh.* About 50 feet down through the woods, I could see the river, and just upstream, the bridge that led to town. What a delightful spot.

"Would you...like to come in?" Ram asked, tentatively.

I itched to have the distraction of Ram's house to keep my mind from Tolly, but unfortunately, Paul's decree echoed through my head.

"Thanks, but I better head home. I like to get to bed nice and early on Fridays so I'm refreshed for my Saturday morning exercise class."

Ever since new year's, I had been doing a great job of

making the gym a regular habit, especially the Saturday morning exercise class.

Ram got out of the car and then turned around and peered back in at me. "Chuli? I'm sorry." And with that, he closed the door and walked to his front door, unlocked it, and went in.

I sat there for a moment, wondering what it meant. Was he sorry for calling my brother? Sorry my brother was evil? Sorry he had invited me in? I really wasn't sure. I backed out of the driveway and headed home for a good cry.

---

seven

• • •

Ram

I COULDN'T STOP THINKING about Chuli. It was bordering on obsession at this point. The way she carried herself, the way she smiled, the way she cared for others, and gods...the way she danced. I was crushing hard.

The more I fell for her, the less I knew what to do about it. She was breaking through my shell somehow, one smile at a time, and making me feel in ways I hadn't felt in...centuries.

I thought back over the years. My soul had been destroyed that day on the cliff, and I had buried the remnants deep inside a shell of hardened focus and determination. It made me unrecognizable, even to myself.

I'd been alone since, shutting out everyone else I cared about, even my brother. I didn't deserve the love, comfort and forgiveness my family would bring.

But seeing Chuli's reaction to her brother made me realize how foolish I had been all these years. Close family was a precious gift. They didn't deserve to be shut out of my life. It wasn't fair to them.

No matter how much I wanted to, I couldn't take away

whatever pain Chuli's brother had put her through in the past, but I could damn well try to mend my own family. What would my little brother say if I called him right now, and told him about my current dilemma? I decided to find out.

---

eight

. . .

Chuli

RAM and I settled into a new routine all this week at work — comfortable silence. I wondered if I had only dreamed up some of the previous tension and hostility coming from him in the first few weeks. He didn't seem to be angry at all, at least around me. He just didn't really talk a lot, and didn't really smile either.

What if I was the one projecting bad vibes the whole time, and he had simply been reacting to it? Was I a total bitch to him at first? I didn't know, but despite Paul's warnings, I found his presence oddly soothing in my office.

This morning, I was reflecting quite a bit on Ram. It was easy enough to do from my vantage point. Lucy had a chiropractor's appointment, so I was working the front of the house for a few hours. I stood behind the counter, and could easily see directly into my office. I reminded myself to never do anything embarrassing in there, as Lucy really could see all.

I looked at the top of Ram's head as he leaned forward, concentrating on his laptop screen. His hair was thick and shiny. *How long was it? Was it as soft as it looked?* I had to admit that I really wanted to touch it, but then stopped that line of thinking right there. Ogling co-workers was a no-no. In Ram's case, especially so. Besides, two men/love interests to ponder over were plenty. *He's just interesting because he's so tight-lipped. He's probably just as normal as everyone else, once you get to know him.*

There was still something fishy going on. But what? Why did normally unflappable Paul hate him so much, despite his insistence that he wasn't the one who dosed me with Veruni?

The most logical theory was that Paul tolerated him for the sake of the website, which was coming along swimmingly. You don't have to like everyone you hire to do a job, right?

For the millionth time, I went over the details of New Year's. Was I ever going to figure out what happened? Was I just a random target, or was someone patiently biding their time, waiting to get to me again? Was The Whisper working on the case right now?

I began to fantasize that he caught the culprit, put him in Immortal jail or whatever, and came back to me, revealing his beautiful true self before embracing me in a passionate kiss, but my reverie was interrupted by the pinging of my phone. It was Zach, sending a picture of a car somewhere in the midwest. He was working his way towards me. *Or maybe he was nearby, and just pretending to be on tour?* I truly didn't know anymore. Maybe he was the one who dosed me, but that didn't make sense either, no matter how many times I mulled it over. Why would he drug a willing subject, and why would he wait so long afterward to even see me?

I wondered yet again if maybe that meant he was The Whisper. *Was he staying away because he was hot on the case?* When he was finally here in person, I had a few tricks up my sleeve to help get to the bottom of this. I would create a whispering game of some kind, or maybe I would just grab him and hug him. I would know the feeling of his body next to mine, and his subtle smell: It was a mix of something earthy and natural, like a forest or a meadow, and something divine, like temples, or sandalwood, mixed in equal proportions.

Perhaps Ram and Zach were just normal dudes, living life, doing their thing. Or maybe Zach was. *Ram was definitely not a normal dude.* Paul wouldn't be so bothered by him if that were the case. He did have some kind of presence, that was for sure.

I looked at him again through the glass. What did I know about him? I suspected he was Hindu, from the way he revered the Ganesha statue at my house, but I couldn't be certain. I thought about the band on his finger again. *Was it a wedding ring? Did Hindus even wear wedding rings? If it was, where was his wife? Was she just at home?* I didn't see enough of his house to know if he lived alone or with a wife and maybe even kids. It was such a small town, I felt certain Lucy would have somehow gotten the dirt on his private life, if there was anything further to know. I'd have to ask her when she came over tonight.

He had said he was from Mathura. I had looked it up a few days later. It was a sacred city in Northern India. It had sounded familiar because it was a pilgrimage site to Hindus and Hare Krishnas. I tried to picture him as a child, running barefoot along the streets, laughing. I closed my eyes and visualized myself there too. I could almost feel the stones under my own feet. The feeling made me smile. I looked at him again. He was still staring at his screen. I thought about Barb and once again, I could almost, but not quite, see the sadness hanging about him. He looked up and caught me staring.

Just like last time, when I had tried to see his aura, his expression softened towards me. It seemed to say "ask me anything. Please."

Should I? *Damn Paul to Hell for forbidding me to get involved.* I was a caring person and more than anything, I wanted to help anyone who needed it, and I felt certain that he needed a friend. I also somehow felt like it was an invitation he was extending only to me. Should I accept it, consequences be damned? It could be a nice distraction from the shambles of my love life.

The bells jingled on the door as someone came in. Before I could force myself to turn away from Ram, I watched him as he broke eye contact with me to see who had come in the door. I stared, spellbound, as his face lit up into a smile even bigger than that glimpse I'd gotten on Valentine's Day. Holy Hell was he adorable when he smiled. *He has dimples! That is the face of an angel!* He jumped up and disappeared from view as he went to the office door to come down to greet whoever had walked in.

I sucked in a breath and turned to face whoever he had smiled at. It was a man wearing sunglasses. He wore very tight, fashionable clothing, indicating he was from the city. He was tall, and his tight hoodie hugged a well-defined chest. He was about 6 feet inside the door. As he looked towards the back where Ram was coming down the few steps, he tossed his hood back and stuck his sunglasses in his pocket.

I froze in shock. Speaking of angel faces, it was none other than Sundar Lal. THE Sundar Lal. Voted most handsome Indian actor for 3 years running, Sundar was a massive force in the Bollywood industry. He was loved by all, including, apparently, Ram. And he was here. In Burning Wind.

"Big Brother!" He bellowed as a devilish grin enveloped his face.

Ram reached him and pulled him in for an embrace. It was almost like watching two mountains colliding. They laughed and teared up as they embraced. It was clear they had a great love for each other, and it was also clear that they hadn't seen each other for a very long time. It was the kind of embrace one would expect to see on a news feature about twins that had been separated since they were children, or family members who had thought the other was dead after a massive earthquake. I was caught up in its beauty and found my own eyes getting misty.

Finally, the two released each other and Ram turned toward me. "Chuli, I'd like you to meet my little brother. He goes by Sundar these days. Sundar, this is my...co-worker, Chuli."

I wasn't sure why he paused before calling me his co-worker. I guess he must've been too embarrassed to call me his boss in front of his brother.

Sundar flashed Ram a look that was hard for me to decipher. *Wonder? Pity?* Ram flashed him a look as well, a much sterner one. It made me feel uncomfortable for a second, until Sundar didn't just look at me again, but he observed me from head to toe, as if he needed to memorize my features. He then gave me the warmest, most loving smile. It made me feel gooey all over. It made me feel totally seen and recognized, as if we were already very dear friends.

He pulled me in for a long, enveloping, tight hug and said "Sister!"

He smelled delicious, and slightly familiar, though I couldn't quite name the smell. I felt wonderful in his arms, so loved, so protected. It was magical. He gently released me, but continued to smile at me. To say I felt flattered would be an understatement.

"Nice to meet you, Sundar. I'm a big fan of your work, especially Mahaan Yuddh." I felt I was doing a pretty good job of completing sentences while I still felt so starstruck.

"You love my work, Sister?" he began to laugh the most beautiful, contagious kind of laughter.

I wanted to laugh with him, although I didn't know what was funny.

"She is not your sister." Uh-oh. Ram's old Scowling Man Bun ways were back — *I hadn't imagined them!*

He was blasting the tension towards his brother at the moment. Instead of being intimidated, however, Sundar just laughed even more.

"Are you trying to frighten me? What a scary pout you've got there. If she's not my sister, then that must mean I'm free to do whatever I'd like with her then, eh?" Sundar winked at me.

Although he was known for being a flirt and was rumored to be romantically involved with several famous actresses and models in the past, I also knew he was recently and very publicly married. I understood that he was only teasing Ram. Besides, I really did have an unexplainable feeling of kinship with him. Fun-sucker wasn't so sure, but she was never going to have a good time teasing anyone anyway, so phooey on her. Ram grew angry at Sundar's flirting.

"You will NOT, brother." Without giving Sundar a moment to apologize, Ram punched him in the gut.

He doubled over for a moment before giving Ram a swift "it's on" kind of glance he was so famous for before the big action scenes in his movies, then he jumped into action.

I backed up a safe distance away from the two brutes as they beat at each other. I had no idea what to do, so I just kind of stood there, most likely with my mouth hanging open. When the fighting got serious enough that they knocked down the incense display, I knew the madness had to stop, however, before the entire store was destroyed.

"YOOOO!" I bellowed and whistled my two fingers in a loud shriek.

They both snapped out of it and stopped, breathing

heavily. Then they helped each other to their feet and righted the toppled display. Amazingly, most of the hanging bags remained in-tact.

"Aww man, my sunglasses!" The broken arm on Sundar's sunglasses seemed to be the most upsetting part about the entire fight to him.

They diligently picked up everything that had fallen. There were a few broken bags, and Sundar placed them on the counter with a $100 bill.

"This should cover anything that broke. Sorry about that, Sister! And I'm sorry for the comment. I shouldn't have joked like that." He walked over to Ram. They gave each other a casual embrace and a kiss on the cheek as if they had not been beating the crap out of each other.

"So good to see you, brother. Dinner tomorrow at my place in the city." Sundar turned to me next. "See you tomorrow, Chuli. I'll send a driver to your place at 5. Bring an overnight bag. Ram, you can ride in with her, so be at her place by then."

We both opened our mouths — mine in shock, but Ram's, apparently, to try to argue. Sundar put his hand out as if to stop him from speaking.

"Radha will never forgive me if I don't introduce her to — your co-worker." He started walking towards the door, then turned with his devilish smirk. "Brother, you're lucky our fight got stopped before you got what you deserved. You're getting weak, old man!" He laughed that beautiful laugh again.

Ram just gave him a "We'll see about that" kind of a look, but with a twinkle in his eye.

"Every moment will be misery until I lay eyes on you again, sweet sister Chuli."

He bowed towards me and then blew me a series of kisses as he headed out the door, right past a stunned Lucy, who had been quietly standing just inside the door for who knows how long.

"Oh, Lucy! How long have you been here?" I gave a warm smile to her.

Her eyes were as big as saucers. "Was...that..." She couldn't even finish her sentence.

"Ram's brother, Sundar," I slowly enunciated every word, with a tone implying *holy shit, yes, that was Sundar Lal and he is Ram's freaking BROTHER and we are soooooo going to talk about this later tonight.*

"And...he...just..." She continued, a hint of mania beginning to peek through.

I continued for her. "Invited me to dinner. To meet Radha."

For once, Lucy was completely tongue-tied. She looked like she couldn't decide if the appropriate response was to scream, throw up, or faint. *I know the feeling!* Sundar and Radha were basically the power couple of Bollywood. Their love was epic, their wedding was epic, their movies were epic. And I was going to dinner with them. And our grumpy computer guy.

Lucy gripped my hands with hers and we exchanged a final we will so dish about this later holy hell look. The moment was interrupted by the sound of my office door closing by Ram. He must've walked away while we were having our secret Bollywood freakout moment.

I gave Lucy one final look and walked back to my office. Ram sat at his desk, once again absorbed in his laptop. I glanced out the glass to the front. Lucy held Sundar's money in her hand as if it were a sacred relic.

"So..." I tried for a casual tone, but I felt like my voice perhaps held a note of hysteria. "Let me just..." I paused again, cleared my throat, and tried to form words one last time. "Can I just, um, review the last few minutes? You know, just to make sure I have the, uh, facts straight?"

Ram turned his attention to my face.

"Ok, so...the biggest star in Bollywood, Sundar Lal, just came here, to Burning Wind. Because he's your long lost brother." I paused.

Ram nodded in a "yep, basically" kind of way.

"And then, your long lost brother, Sundar Lal, beat you up, and arranged a double date tomorrow, so I can meet India's Sweetheart, Radha Lal."

"He did NOT beat me up! I beat HIM up, obviously. And it's not a date." He aimed for his usual stern tone, but it felt lighter somehow, as if he was infected with the same warmth Sundar had somehow spread to me.

I walked closer to where he sat as I looked at his lopsided bun and disheveled appearance, and gave him a skeptical look as I playfully reached out and gently touched the puffy, bruised skin around his swollen eye with the tips of my fingers. "Sure he didn't."

He flinched slightly at my touch, but then stayed very still. I slowly, delicately dragged my hand down the side of his face as I removed it. I couldn't help it. It was remarkable how soft and warm his skin was. My hand now hung awkwardly by my side, useless, like it no longer served a purpose.

What had been meant as a teasing gesture suddenly changed the air in the room around us. We stayed frozen in place, staring at each other again. How did this keep happening? Once again, I felt myself swept up in his pleading gaze. I wanted to ask him so much. My hand was inching up my side again. It was just about to touch him when my phone buzzed and dinged in my pocket, making me jump a little bit. It was Paul. I took a deep breath, stepped back from Ram, and turned to answer.

"Hi-ya Paul!" I mustered up the least guilty, most nonchalant hello I could.

Maybe it was better that he had interrupted. *Yes, it defi-*

nitely was, I told myself. We chatted about an upcoming book release, and it helped dispel whatever weird magic was in the air. I blamed Sundar. Clearly, his presence had affected us both.

When I got off the phone, I headed back down to the store to help Lucy clean up the last of the damage and finalize our plans for the night before she left. Occasionally, I'd glance up through the glass again. I swore I could feel Ram's eyes on me, but every time I looked up, he was busily engaged in his laptop. Ram and I both gathered our belongings and prepared to head out the door. Inwardly, I was listing all the reasons why it was absolutely essential I didn't obsess over Ram, and insisting to myself that tomorrow was NOT a date; Ram had said so himself.

As we walked out the door, he spoke. "You ok?"

"Me? Uh, yeah, sorry, I'm just...uh, thinking about that book release."

It was a lame excuse, but it was better than "just having a chat with myself about all the reasons not to obsess over you."

"Are YOU ok? You better get some ice on that eye so you can see me with it tomorrow!"

He gave me a sweet little smile. "This," he pointed at his eye, which admittedly already looked less swollen, "is nothing. I'm a fast healer."

I smiled and waved and began trudging up the street.

---

nine

. . .

Chuli

A LIGHT TAPPING SOUNDED at the door. The cautious new me, who somehow kept finding myself in crazy situations, had finally become wary enough to ask who was at the door first instead of just throwing it open.

"It's Ram," His voice was softened through the layers of the old pine door.

I unlocked it, opened it a tad, and then stood back to allow him room to enter. He slipped inside and closed the door behind him before looking at me. His eyes flared with a bit of something. I thought perhaps it was a look of surprise.

"Chuli, you look…" He took in my sequined dress and boots.

After much discussion with Lucy last night, we determined that since New Year's Eve had been a bust, I may as well drag this outfit back out of retirement. I felt great in it, and it fit me like a second skin. We figured it was the best outfit I owned to go meet movie stars for dinner while feeling at least a little good about myself. He never did finish his sentence. Instead, he just looked down, slightly bashful.

"Thanks, I think. You also...look," I laughed. "How's that eye today?" I stepped a little closer to peer at the swollen, tender place I had touched yesterday, but to my surprise, there was nothing there but a tiny trace of a shadow, like it never happened.

I was definitely confused and surprised. *I definitely did NOT want to touch that spot again, just for comparison.* I tucked my hand into a fist to tell it to not even think about engaging in any funny business.

Ram shrugged his shoulders a little and said, "I told you, I'm a fast healer."

"Well damn Ram, you should write a book! You can call it, Heal Thyself the IT Way. I know a great little publisher that might just be willing to print it, especially if your technique involves magic spells or crystals."

He smiled a bit at this, a quick burst of sun between clouds. Before I could dwell over all the reasons why I needed to not be doing any marveling at all, and why he was a total jerk, just as Lucy and I had discussed in our "pros and cons of Ram vs Zach" last night, he interrupted my thoughts.

"Car's here, you ready?"

I grabbed my coat and a small overnight bag, just in case, as Sundar had suggested. The ride was comfortable. It was a large, dark SUV with tinted windows. I was impressed by the comfort of the seats and the little cooler and basket attached to the seats in front of us, filled with possibly every kind of snack that rich people feasted on. Fancy mineral waters, organic almonds, date bars — it was all there.

"So this is how the other half lives," I mused.

This was the nicest ride I ever took. Ram didn't seem particularly impressed or enthusiastic about the car. Maybe this was how he and his brother were raised. *But if that were the case, why didn't Ram have a nice car now? Stop thinking about Ram.* I had wanted to pore over the entertainment websites to read about Sundar's childhood. It would have been a great opportunity to learn more about Ram's past as well, but ultimately, it felt too creepy and invasive, and besides, I was NOT trying to find out more information about Ram. *Ugh.*

After a final longing look at the rich people snacks, I reluctantly declined them too, just in case. I couldn't forget to be on my guard. I was already inwardly freaking out, trying to figure out how to not eat or drink at dinner tonight. *Perhaps I'll just push my food around the plate?* I leaned against the back of the seat and sighed.

"They're safe," Ram assured me.

"Who's safe?" I asked, confused.

Ram gestured towards the cooler. "Sundar is a very famous celebrity. He has a security team dedicated to keeping him and Radha safe from any potential threat, including...illness."

"Who said I was afraid to eat or drink?" I asked him suspiciously.

"I sit next to you every day. You think I haven't noticed that you always bring your own lunch and water bottle? You decline every offer to go out for food or drinks that comes your way. Also, I heard you tell Lucy you had food poisoning over New Year's. Therefore, I think it's safe to assume you have fear related to food and drink."

Damn, I thought, *he might be a jerk, but he's an observant jerk.* I supposed he was right though. Perhaps I was in a safe place where I could finally let my guard down a little. I grabbed an Italian mineral water and a paleo bar made of blueberries, nuts, and dates. It tasted like heaven compared to the same boring salads, smoothies and hummus wraps I'd been eating for weeks now.

When I was done savoring every last bite and sitting contentedly against the back of the seat, Ram spoke.

"Did you have fun with Lucy last night?"

I thought about last night. It was fun. It had been nice to do some good old-fashioned girl talking. "It was...really nice."

Unfortunately, I hadn't been able to truly dish all of my thoughts and problems, since I didn't feel it was right or safe to tell Lucy about The Whisper and new year's and the Veruni, and especially the Valentine's Day kiss, and Lucy seemed strangely tight-lipped about her night with Gustov.

Instead, it had turned into a Zach vs. Ram extravaganza. Zach, barring anything crazy different about him in person, had eventually won out over Ram, because he was so charming and polite and dreamy on the phone, and Ram was so stern and grumpy and uncaring. Except for right now, when he seemed like he really did care if I had a nice night with Lucy. *Stop thinking about Ram. Stop stop stop.*

Ram nodded. I managed to change the subject to something more neutral, and after a brief discussion on the timeline for the live debut on the website next week, the rest of the ride passed in silence. Instead of irritating me, Ram was beginning to be a steady presence I felt quite used to under all his bristling, and I was going to miss him when the website was built. *Shit. You're doing it again. Stop!*

Finally, we arrived. The Lal's temporary house was a beautiful townhome in Manhattan. Ram was correct when he talked about the heightened level of security. When I got out of the car and stretched my legs, I quickly scanned the street and noticed security guards discreetly stationed near any potential entrance. I would have felt completely relaxed if it wasn't for the butterflies in my stomach. *I was about to see Sundar and Radha Lal!*

All my fears dissipated, however, when the door opened wide, and Sundar's famous smile greeted us. I couldn't help but smile back. He took turns giving each of us a warm hug in greeting. Once again, I found myself not wanting to let go of him. *How did he do that?* He smelled so delicious and familiar, and hugging him made everything right with the world. I did let go, however, when I heard the sound of footsteps running down the stairs. Radha came flying down with the biggest, brightest smile, a smile that perhaps outshone her husband's.

"Big Brother!!" She yelped, jumping directly into the arms of Ram. He was taken a bit by surprise, but seemed happy to see her as well.

"Hey, little sis!" He set her down while she wiped away tears of joy.

"We've missed you so much — don't ever go away this long ever again!"

He seemed bashful, or possibly ashamed, and gave her an apologetic smile and he wiped at his eyes.

Radha's gaze turned on me. I'd been obscured from her vision by Sundar. She gave me a rapturous look of awe. I felt as if I were a beautiful statue or vision from heaven. I was amazed that anyone could respond to me that way, let alone two movie stars on two separate days. *What is even happening in my life?!* I thought, as fresh tears welled in Radha's eyes.

"Sister!" she cried out, then she pulled me into a fierce, passionate, hug.

It turned out the tears were contagious. I found my own eyes welling up, though I'd no idea why. Maybe it was because the last time I had been in a woman's arms, it had been my mother's, as we cried tears of goodbye at the monastery. She was so soft and nice, and she too smelled delicious.

Ram cleared his throat, probably in an attempt to move things past crying in the doorway. "Radha, this is Chuli. She is my co-worker."

He seemed to love the word co-worker. Radha let go of me, but immediately intertwined my hand with her own, as if we were childhood friends.

"I am aware. C'mon Chuli, let me show you around! And then you can tell me everything about you!" And with that, she pulled me through the doorway and around the whole house for a grand tour of their spacious digs.

For some inexplicable reason, the two of us already felt like two peas in a pod, and I knew in my heart of hearts that I could truly relax here and be myself without fear. After struggling with so much fear and anxiety and uncertainty so far this year, it was a relief to cast it aside for a moment. Now the future seemed full of promise.

The tour concluded in the largest, most perfectly organized closet I'd ever seen. Row upon row of clothes for every occasion donned rack after rack. My phone pinged in my hand, and I excused myself from Radha for a moment to answer. It was Zach, of course. I opened the picture he sent. It was the front of Burning Wind Press! My stomach gave a nervous flutter. *Zach was in my town?* He wasn't supposed to meet up with me until next week. A text quickly followed.

> Looky what I found! My last convention got canceled, so I thought I'd surprise you with an early visit. :) You home?

Ugh. Why did this picture make me feel more disturbed and stressed out than happy? That couldn't be right. I was supposed to be looking forward to meeting him.

Radha must've seen the look of concern on my face. She took my hand again. "Something wrong, sister?"

"No. Well....kind of," and I opened up to Radha. The words just came pouring out.

I didn't mention anything about magic potions or whispers, but I did give the background scoop on Zach, on our longtime flirting, our canceled plans, and how I was having misgivings, but I wasn't sure what to do.

No offense to Lucy, but our list of pros and cons had only really skimmed the surface of basic character traits and flaws we were aware of. We didn't really get into the intricacies of my actual feelings and emotions, so it hadn't really helped me figure out exactly how to handle the Zach situation. Radha offered me some advice.

"You need to meet him in person. Once you do, you'll know. Especially if you let him kiss you. When Sundar kissed me, I knew right then and there that he was the only man for me, no matter what else came between us." She smiled a dreamy smile. It was the smile of a woman deeply satisfied. It was beautiful to behold.

I remembered seeing a face very similar to that smiling back at me in Paul's mirror, after I'd been kissed by The Whisper on Valentine's Day. *Could Zach really be The Whisper?* If I could confirm that, I knew I could feel as confident about him as Radha felt about Sundar.

I smiled and thanked her, and told her that was perfect advice. She seemed pleased. I texted Zach with apologies for being out of town, though I had to admit to myself, I wasn't sorry in the slightest.

I suggested he get a room at the Inn, and we could go for a hike tomorrow in the mountains behind town. That would be a perfect date. It didn't involve food, but it did involve exercise, which meant I could skip my early morning workout at the gym and not feel guilty about it. He agreed to the plan, and I set my phone down after switching it off.

We were still in Radha's incredible closet, and my eyes were drawn to a section dedicated to gorgeous, sparkling saris, the large decorative Indian cloth women pleated around themselves when dressed for special occasions.

Radha delicately touched them. "You like saris?" She asked me, intrigued.

"I've always admired them. They're so beautiful! They

look very complicated. How do you keep them from falling off?"

Radha tried to explain, but ultimately determined it was easier to demonstrate. She made me undress, and gave me a petticoat and short blouse to wear. She wrapped the sari around me, teaching me where to pleat and where to tuck. It was tricky, but I eventually got the hang of it, despite Fun-sucker's frustration at my struggles.

Radha backed up to look at me. "Your hair…" She gestured to my two plain braids, "it's... Can I play with it?"

I knew she was politely trying to say that my hair was way too plain to match up with such a gorgeous outfit, but I wasn't offended. She was right. And if Radha Lal, queen of Bollywood fashion, wanted to play makeover, who was I to stop her?! I nodded enthusiastically.

She sat me down at her organized vanity facing away from the mirror, and took my braids out, combed her fingers through my hair, and got to work. She gave me a simple half-up style, complete with a beautiful piece of golden jewelry hung from the part. Radha called it maang tika. We giggled like schoolgirls at Radha's attempts to get it to hang properly. It was such fun, and something I never thought I'd enjoy. *This must be what it feels like to have a sister.* I quickly shut down that line of thinking, as it was only going to lead to sorrow and self-pity that my only sibling was a brother that hated me. I was here now, and Radha was here, and this was a beautiful moment. I was going to embrace it.

Radha pulled me up from my seat and stood me in front of the full-length mirror. "Oooooh…sister," Radha half-whispered, in awe.

I felt a mix of emotions staring at myself in the mirror. I felt beautiful and powerful, familiar, but not. *Is that really me?* I thought of my father and my Lenape heritage, and felt a pang of guilt at how good I felt in this foreign get-up.

"It's probably almost time for dinner. I should get change..." Before I could finish my sentence, Sundar and Ram walked in through the open door.

"Hey you two! Read..." Sundar's words died in his throat as our eyes locked through the mirror. He absent-mindedly wrapped his arm around Radha, who had snuggled up next to him. The most famous face in India looked absolutely starstruck as he took me in.

I looked at Ram, who had stopped just inches from the door. He seemed to have a mix of emotions on his face, none of them good, however.

"I was just going to get changed," I stated quietly, in an effort to pierce through the tense silence that had just permeated the room.

Ram's face fixed into a cold, steely glare that he turned on Radha as if to say *How dare you*. He turned on his heel and marched out of the room. Sundar flashed her an apologetic smile and trailed after him.

"Did I...do something wrong?" I felt like I did, but how could a harmless game of dress-up be a bad thing?

"No, no, no sister! This is not your fault. It is mine. Why don't you get changed while I go fix it?" She gave me a peck on the cheek and headed out the door, to right whatever wrong had just happened.

I got changed as fast as I could, then got down on the floor to eavesdrop on the conversation below that was filtering through the floorboards. It seemed like a logical way to get to the bottom of whatever was happening. I couldn't hear everything they were saying, but I understood enough to know that Ram was trying to leave, and they were trying to stop him.

His voice got louder in frustration. "She's just my co-worker for this stupid job I don't even like! I can't wait for it to end. Being there next to her every day is already torture, and then you invite her here with us, like she's family, and then you go and dress her up like a BRIDE!? Do you have ANY idea how painful that is to see? I can't. Be. Around. Her. Just let me leave!"

Sundar was saying something quieter back to Ram, but I couldn't listen anymore. I slumped onto the floor. The karmic sting for eavesdropping was a harsh one indeed. I felt tears stinging my eyes. I knew Ram was jaded and arrogant, but I'd been assuming it was a mask that hid a sensitive, sweet soul beneath. Apparently, I'd badly misjudged him. It was actually hiding a viper. He was so disgusted by me that it physically pained him to be in my presence, and he was counting down the minutes until I could be out of his life for good. My chest felt heavy, and I felt trapped here, curled up on the floor. I needed a plan to get out of here. *Should I fake an illness?*

I never wanted to see Ram ever again. Radha quietly crept through the door and sat down next to me, lightly placing her hand on my back. "You heard him?"

I slowly nodded, my face buried in my hands. My whole life, I had gone out of my way to make sure I was liked by all. It was probably because of my brother, but I couldn't stand the fact that anyone else would think anything bad of me, let alone say cruel things about me loudly to others after being nice to me moments before. The resemblance to Tolly was too much to bear right now, and the tears would not be stopped.

"I'm a..nice...person, I swear," I stammered out between sobs that threatened to overtake me. "Why...do they..hate me?"

Radha lifted my head up and into her lap, comforting me. "Shhhh...no one could ever hate you. You are absolutely perfect."

She stroked my hair off my tear-stained face as I cried. "Ram didn't mean what he said. He has never been one to deal with the finer side of emotions. Deep down, he is just a hurt and scared little boy. It's only natural when you've been hurt as badly as him. I think seeing you like that brought up feelings for him that he likes to keep buried."

"What happened to him?" I had wondered so many times. *Would I finally get some answers?* The intrigue, combined with Radha's tender care, was enough to help slowly bring me out of my pity party.

Radha hesitated. "It's not really my place to say,"

"Radha, please. Clearly something has happened to him. I've been dying to know what. Maybe I can face him better if I understand. Otherwise, I don't know if I'll ever be able to face him again." This was the absolute truth, and Radha knew it.

Reluctantly, she began. "Ram was married at an early age. I wouldn't say they were the happiest couple, but often arranged marriages are like that. It takes time to get to know each other. They had their disagreements, but it seemed like deep down, they loved and respected each other. That's why it was such a shock to us all…" Radha trailed off, a sad look on her beautiful features.

"What shock?"

Radha looked pained to continue. "No one knows for sure what happened. Ram was away and got delayed somehow. By the time he returned home, she was…gone."

"What do you mean, gone?" We were whispering now.

"She was last seen walking near the cliffs. They say she…jumped."

I let out a breath at the words. *Suicide*. Barb had nailed it.

"When Ram found out," Radha wiped tears away, "distraught doesn't begin to cover it. He refused to believe it. He left, determined to get her back somehow. This is the first we've seen him since. It's been ages. But now…" Radha paused, unsure what to say next.

As awful as he had just made me feel, I felt my heart

break for him just the same. Sundar walked in the room.

"Everything ok?" he asked tenderly.

The two of us straightened up. "Yep, just fine. We'll, uh, be down in a few," I tried my best for a stoic look.

Sundar gave me a sympathetic one back.

"Is Ram staying, love?" Radha asked him.

"I guilted him into it."

"Good. See you downstairs then."

Sundar left and we stood up. I went to the vanity and looked at myself in the mirror. Puffy, red-rimmed eyes, a splotchy face, and frizzy hair greeted me in return. *How am I going to go face the public with the hottest couple in India like this?* As if she could read my thoughts, Radha dug through her vanity drawers and pulled out a small blue bottle with a gold label with four letters on it: IDUN. She smiled.

"Let's get you cleaned up, eh?" She poured a few drops of oil from the bottle into her hands, rubbed them together, and delicately applied the oil to my face, closed eyes, and hair.

It felt and smelled wonderful, like the essence of an apple orchard on a misty morning. I opened my eyes and looked in the mirror and was completely shocked at the transformation. *No wonder Radha and Sundar looked so good, with access to expensive beauty products like whatever this magic oil is!*

I still looked like myself, only it was like myself on my best day. All traces of redness and swelling vanished. I looked fresh and dewy, like I had slept 8 perfect hours, drank plenty of water, and had just gotten back from hot yoga class and had a green smoothie. I practically glowed. *And my hair!* It was now smooth, glossy, and shiny, with not a frizz in sight.

"Oh my god…" I began to exclaim.

"Goddess, you mean!" Radha winked at me, grabbed my hand, and we headed downstairs.

Before we left, Ram pulled me aside. "I owe you an apology," he stated, eyes at the floor. "I was rude, and it wasn't your fault."

I stared at him. "Thanks," I said. "I'm not, by the way."

"Not what?" he asked, looking at me for a moment before quickly looking away again.

It really does pain him to look at me.

"Trying to be your bride."

He looked at me with an indecipherable look before I walked away.

We strolled down the street, to a tiny vegan restaurant that was apparently reserved just for us. I noticed more bodyguards stationed around, and felt safe enough to eat, but not quite at ease.

I understood a little bit more about Ram now, and that he was a deeply hurt, grieving mess inside, but I also knew he didn't want to be around me at all, and I couldn't help but feel hurt by that. I tried my best to avoid him, but it was pretty difficult, given the intimate circumstances.

Sundar and Radha led the conversation, and they did a damn fine job of it. They were both so lovely and charming, and soon I really was feeling at ease. I began opening up to their questions more and more. I explained what it was like to be a child before and then after a divorce. I told them how I still missed my Dad every day, and how I tried to handle the mixed emotions of being happy for my mom that she had finally found her right place, but how much I missed her companionship. I briefly mentioned my brother, but Radha and Sundar were both excellent at social cues, so they expertly steered the subject to something less difficult.

Ram was quiet and polite, but never chimed in, even when Sundar told a few stories from their escapades as children. When Sundar asked him direct questions about work and how he wound up in the IT field, Ram used only the most general terms, claiming the nuts and bolts of computer systems were boring, and difficult to explain. Sundar laughed at this and readily agreed, but I sensed that it hurt him to see his brother so reserved and unhappy.

The conversation veered to romance and relationships. I told them about several failed attempts at dating in college, but how I never quite seemed to find anyone that felt right for me. I swore to them I believed in love and that I was a big fan of it, believing in my heart of hearts that everyone has at least one person in the universe that's perfect for them — maybe even more than one — but that I had yet to personally experience it for myself.

I had a brief flash of The Whisper kissing me in the closet and deep down suspected I had the beginnings of that experience, but that didn't quite seem like polite dinner conversation, so I left it unspoken.

"Maybe it will happen as early as tomorrow," Radha winked at me.

"Tomorrow? Do tell!" Sundar feigned great enthusiasm. "I suspect Radha knows a little something that we don't."

"Well...I may have mentioned my date tomorrow," I explained. I wasn't planning on bringing it up, but maybe it was a good thing to talk about. *In fact,* I thought, *maybe it will be a big context clue to Ram that he has nothing to fear from me, and I'm not gunning to become his next bride.* Perhaps it would make our last week together slightly more comfortable.

"Who's the lucky soul who gets to court the lovely Chuli Davis?" Sundar teased.

I told them about Zach, and about my misgivings, but how Radha and I had determined it was best to just meet him in person to see. This led to a lengthy discussion about the strange new world of internet dating.

Could someone really get to know someone else without ever seeing them in person? Did brains fill in the blanks wrong, creating a false persona that was nothing like the actual person? What if that person had annoying traits in real life? Did one have to be more or less cautious when planning a date like this?

This led to a lengthy debate about safety. I assured them that I carried pepper spray in my bag and a penknife in my pocket at all times, and that I was going to text Paul my itinerary and share my location so that someone would know immediately if I went missing. Radha and Sundar both agreed that I was being smart. Ram, of course, didn't say anything at all. He just kept his head down.

As we ate our way through several courses, I realized just how much I missed and needed this kind of companionship in my life. True, I had Paul and Stewie, but our friendship had fallen into more of the work-talk, day-to-day things over the last few years, rather than discussing the deep stuff, our conversation about New Year's Eve notwithstanding. *Perhaps I should have done a better job at keeping in touch with friends from college,* I thought. But with my extreme dislike of social media, I rarely heard from any of them, except an occasional birth announcement or wedding invitation. They all seemed to be caught up in the "real world", while I plugged away bringing the mystical and the occult to the fringe members of society.

I had thought I was perfectly happy doing this, but for the first time, a new awareness crept in. *Stagnation.* I quickly tamped it back down and shut the door on it. *My job is my life, and it's going to stay that way, damn it!* Paul needed me, and that was that.

When dinner was finally over, we walked back up the street to the house. I declined to spend the night. I did not want to ruin this evening with the inevitable nightmares that would arrive, so we all gave each other warm and sweet embraces goodbye and promised to stay in touch. Radha and I exchanged phone numbers.

The SUV pulled up, and Ram and I climbed inside. The ride home was quiet. Ram didn't speak at all, and I spent my time replaying some of the more interesting conversations from the evening, trying not to fall asleep in the plush, comfortable seat. I thought I was doing well in the last regard, until out of nowhere, there was a large, stern hand, shaking my shoulder.

"Mmmmmmmm," I purred.

I had been having such a lovely dream. I pulled at some threads to try to remember the specifics while curling up, my arms draped around warmth. I was almost back in the dream when I was shaken again.

"Chuli…wake up, damn it."

Slowly, I started to come to. I went to wipe a stray hair off my face that was tickling me when I realized exactly where I was and what I was doing. I had fallen asleep, and fallen over, with my head and hands sprawled all over Ram's lap. *Holy Hell.*

I sat up so quickly I nearly smacked my head on the door. "Ram! I am so sorry…"

I was absolutely mortified; he was equally so. He quickly placed his hands in the lap I had just vacated. Just then, the driver opened my car door, nearly spilling me out of it.

"Here we are then, safe and sound," he said, oblivious to the situation in the car.

I scrambled out the door as fast as I could, fumbled with my keys, and went inside, locking the door behind me.

---

ten

. . .

Chuli

I am watching the fight from above. The huge beast is angry, clawed talons swiping at the ground. She has been terrorizing the town, and has killed dozens so far.

He has her trapped along a dead-end street. She lunges toward him, but he deftly moves out of the way. He spins his weapon high above his head, gaining momentum, waiting until the right moment, and delivers a killing blow.

The townspeople, mostly gathered on rooftops like me, cheer and celebrate. I climb down the ladder to congratulate him. When I reach the bottom, I look at him. His jewelry sparkles in the sun, and his bronze skin glistens with sweat. He has his hair half up, with a golden crown on top.

We lock eyes, and everyone else fades away. He has eyes only for me. He stalks towards me. His mouth crashes into mine in a fierce, carnal kiss, as if to say, "Mine."

He lifts me off the ground and into his arms. He begins walking us toward the entrance to the house. His kisses deepen as he takes me over to the bed and begins unwrapping the sari wound around me, tossing it aside.

He looks at me as if I'm the most beautiful creature he's ever seen as he slowly removes his crown and peels his armor off, revealing the massive expanse of his strong, muscular chest and torso. He begins to untie his….

I WOKE UP GASPING, whipping myself into an upright sitting position.

"Gaaaaaaaah! Not HIM! Anyone but him!" I cried out, but there was no one there to reply. I was in my own bed, after all.

The logical side of me knew that dreams were just the brain moving short-term learning to long-term storage, so clearly, the combination of Bollywood stars, exotic food, and the cringe-worthy episode in the car last night had combined in quite an interesting way. Fun-sucker, who had now become completely unreliable as a conscience, begged for me to go back to sleep and finish that dream.

"NO." I sternly told her. "Ugh. Now I'm even having conversations with myself out loud!" I had no response to that.

I glanced at the clock. It was 9:30, the latest I'd slept in on a Saturday in quite some time. *I should really text Zach and finalize our hiking plan,* I thought, but I wasn't sure I could talk to him until I got that awful dream out of my head.

Ram just might be the only man I'd ever met who was physically pained to be in my presence. *Why did it have to be about him?* I didn't want to think of him that way at all. Not even a little bit. *But damn, was he really all buff like that?* I shook my head as if to shake the image back out.

"No, no, no, Chuli, we're not going to go there. We're locking that dream up and throwing away the key." I figured I may as well continue to talk to myself. I was on a roll.

I took a deep breath and climbed out of bed, thinking a shower might help cool me down. After a very long and invigorating one, I was feeling ready to face Zach, so we finalized the plans via text. I was going to meet him in the lobby of the Inn in 30 minutes.

I got dressed in warm layers. Mr. Richards had warned me yesterday that a bitter cold front was moving in at some point today, so I wanted to be properly prepared.

Radha's cream had some lingering effects, I deduced as I looked in the mirror, because I still looked really darn good. I would definitely have to ask Radha where to get some. *It might be worth handing over one or two paychecks for.*

I sent a quick text message to Paul, explaining the date was happening a week early, gave him our hiking route, and shared my phone location.

He sent me a quick "Good luck!"

I headed out the door for the brisk 15-minute walk to the Inn. During my walk, my thoughts kept trying to sneak back to Ram. I was relieved the website was almost done. *I am not going to miss him,* I assured myself. I was not going to miss these weird feelings he brings up. Everything would be easier with him gone.

Things appeared pretty normal as far as anyone attempting to drug me. It was already nearly March, and there was no sign of anything suspicious.

After finally having an evening where I felt free to finally leave my guard down, trying to put those walls back up felt exhausting, and I was eager to find a way to move on. *Was it possible if I never found closure?*

Now, here I was, staring at the front of the Inn, dealing with all of those feelings on top of the usual nervousness that goes along with a first date. *Once he kisses you, you'll just know.* Radha's words played in my head. *What if it was awful?*

I loathed confrontation and causing anyone stress, but here I was, putting myself in another situation that could end with someone being very unhappy with me. I closed my eyes for a moment, took a deep, steadying breath, and went into the lobby.

"Big Bird!"

I turned to my left, in the direction the voice had come from. He was here, and he was just as handsome in real life as in his pictures. *Oh boy.* He seemed so confident and happy to see me. I smiled and headed over towards him. He picked me up and spun me in a circle before gently setting me back down while saying something about me being a sight for sore eyes.

The movement was so fast and unexpected that I forgot to pay attention to his scent, or how our bodies fit together.

He gathered his jacket and hat from a nearby chair and put them on, then intertwined our arms and said, "Shall we stroll, my lady?"

As we started walking up the road that wound past the Chateau and dead-ended at the entrance to the hiking trails that went up the mountain behind town, we made small talk. I decided that Zach was exactly the type of person they would cast in a Hallmark movie when they needed a love interest that was secretly a dashing prince from a small fictional kingdom. He was funny, sweet, charming, and strong. He had lifted me in the lobby with ease.

I tried to get a good reading on his character, a skill I thought I was good at until lately. Ram's secret hatred of me when I thought we were becoming friends was messing with my confidence big time. I kept second-guessing myself. He was so charming, however, one thing I knew for certain: He wasn't someone that needed to drug women.

He seemed much more content to talk about himself rather than ask me questions about myself. It was the opposite of last night's dinner. I brushed it off as nerves. *Even dashing, charming secret princes get nervous sometimes, right?*

We continued to follow the steep trail that wound around the mountain top. He took several opportunities to "help me" along the way — a hand on my back, a light grip on my arm. I felt certain at some point along this hike, he was going to try to kiss me.

I tried to picture him as The Whisper, with his lips on mine. When I did so, an image of Ram from last night's dream came popping out unbidden instead.

"Phbleh!" I said in disgust, as if I could spit the image off my lips.

Zach turned around and gave me a concerned look.

"Sorry. I just got a leaf, or fuzzy or something in my mouth." I pulled my glove off and pretended to remove something from my mouth.

Zach stared at my lips while I did it. *Oh yes, he definitely wants to kiss me.* I smiled and put my glove back on.

"Almost there!" I said, and picked up the pace, leading us to the rocky outcropping near the top of the mountain that revealed the wooded expanse of the mountains and river below.

I stopped about 20 feet from the edge. "This is as far as I go."

Zach looked at me curiously. "You afraid of heights, Big Bird?"

"Something like that," I admitted. "I don't mind being up high, I just don't really like the edge."

Especially today, I thought, remembering the tale of Ram's wife. *What kind of pain must a person be in to willingly jump off something like this?*

"It's OK," he said, coming to stand in front of me. "I like this view better anyway."

He took his gloved finger and touched my face with it. *Ooh, here we go, time for the kiss,* I thought. His face got closer to mine. So far he didn't smell like The Whisper, but it was quite windy up here, so it was impossible to smell him either way.

I closed my eyes, and parted my lips slightly and

waited. And waited more. Nothing. I opened my eyes to see that he had turned his face away, and was taking in the view. *Huh? He's going to drag this out. Damn it!*

"Ready to head back? I'm a tad frozen, and unfortunately, I have to get back to the city tonight. Could I walk you home?"

I agreed. *Maybe he wanted to wait until we were in the warmth?* We headed back down the mountain. This time, he held my hand the entire way, but it was impossible to feel what his hand actually felt like in mine, thanks to our gloves.

There was definitely more focus on the terrain and less chatter on the way down. When we were almost back to the road, we took a brief detour so I could show him the cool old mine tunnel I had discovered.

We peered through the slats of the boards blocking the entrance, our bodies very close to each other, using our flashlight phones to sneak a glimpse inside. Then we headed back out of the woods and into town.

I invited him in from the cold when we got back to my house. I removed my hat, gloves, and coat, but he only took off his gloves and hat, indicating he wasn't planning on staying long. I gave him a brief tour, but my place was so small, it only took a minute. It was cute how many things he remembered from our text messages.

I laughed as he told me how he had pictured the layout versus the actuality, and how he had expected me to have a much nicer blender for my smoothies than the junky old one that graced my countertop. A quick look at the time revealed he was going to be late if he didn't get going soon, so I walked him to the door.

"I'm so sorry I can't stay this time. I promise you that next time, I'll give you all the time in the world. Would you like an eternal date, Big Bird?"

I laughed and said something like "sounds fun," but I

was more interested in what his moves were in this very instant. He was very close to me again. *This is it! It's happening!* This time, I kept my eyes open. He was staring at my lips and was now only inches away. He slowly, slowly, began to close the gap.

BAM! BAM! BAM!

Loud banging on the door startled both of us, since we were standing directly in front of it. *Gods damn it! What NOW?* I thought.

Zach let out a chuckled sigh as he backed away from me. "Sounds important."

"Who is it?" I called out, but inside, I knew exactly who it was.

"It's Ram."

I turned and gave Zach an eye roll. He gave me a *who?* Kind of glance. I thought about explaining, but there wasn't time. Ram was banging again, so I whipped open the door.

"What?" I was shorter than I meant to be, but gods! *Did he really have to show up right now?*

He stood in the doorway and seemed to take up the entire thing, especially compared to Zach's smaller frame. I glanced at his chest. I told myself it was because it just happened to be at my eye level and it had nothing to do with that stupid dream, thank you very much.

"You forgot this last night." He handed me the overnight bag with spare clothes I brought to the city last night, just in case.

Zach looked between the two of us. *Shit. Does he think Ram was my date last night?* Well he had been, but certainly not like that.

"Zach, this is Ram. He is my co-worker." I emphasized the word in much the same way Ram had yesterday. "He's building the new website that's almost ready to launch. Ram, Zach here is one of our best selling authors. He's just passing through on a book tour."

What came next was nearly a replay of what had happened with Gustov. Zach held his hand out in greeting, and Ram just continued to glower from the doorway. This time, his hands were clenched in fists. I pictured the weapon from my dream in one of them. It seemed entirely fitting.

"Ok, well, thanks then. See you Monday." Without giving him a chance to say anything else, I closed the door in his face. He stood there for a moment longer, then his footsteps faded as he walked away.

"Scowling Man Bun, obviously. I didn't picture him to be quite so…" Zach said, trailing off.

"Scowly? Man Bunny?" I suggested.

Zach laughed. "He is definitely no bunny."

We stood there for one more awkward second before Zach gave me a quick peck on the cheek, opened the door, and said, "Goodbye, Chuli. I'll see you in eternity!" And he strolled away.

---

eleven

. . .

Chuli

I STALKED around my living room, frustrated as hell. I was hoping today would be a day of clarification, where I could get a good grip on what was happening in my romantic life. Instead, I was no closer to knowing who The Whisper was, and no closer to knowing if I should continue this thing with Zach.

I was also very, very angry with Ram. First, he had to infiltrate my dreams, and then my date?! *How dare he?! And how DID he?* I became quite suspicious. How did Ram know that I was home? I had mentioned I'd be out on a hiking date during the day. The timing couldn't be a coincidence.

I checked in with Paul, replying to his "how did it go?" with a shrugging shoulders emoji. I was turning off my shared location with him when a thought struck. I went into my contacts and looked at Ram's info. Sure enough, my location was being shared with him as well! That sneaky bastard must've taken my phone and messed with it while I was asleep in the car. He had seemed concerned about my safety last night, but this was crossing a big, red line. I turned off my location and then went one step further, blocking him completely. *If he has anything else to say to me, he can say it in person at the office on Monday.* I certainly had quite a bit to tell him on Monday, and it involved words like "stalker" and "boundaries" and "how fucking dare you?"

I turned to my bag next. *Did Ram plant a tracking device in there too?* I rooted through it, but what I found in there filled me with delight. I pulled out a little blue bottle with a golden label. Radha had scribbled in the margins around the IDUN letters, "Secret weapon for the Goddess Chuli. Miss you Already! Oxoxoxoxox" I sat back and smiled. Finally, something was going right today!

Sunday was a much better day. Mr. Richards and I spent time together eliminating the knocking noises the pipes had begun to make whenever the heat kicked on in my place. We meticulously removed the air from every radiator, and it was running like a dream. It felt so good to have a problem I could solve!

The back and forth problem solving we were doing reminded me so much of my childhood, and fixing broken things with my dad, that I even invited the Richards over for dinner. It was a bit tricky to get Mrs. Richards' wheelchair in the door, but once she was in, we had a lovely meal together. I tried to get them to open up about their past — how they met, interesting places they'd been — but it never seemed to lead anywhere. Mostly we discussed the bitter cold, and how it was called a "polar vortex", and it was set to stay here all week.

Sadly, it was increasingly obvious that Mrs. Richards' mental state was deteriorating. I was pretty sure Mr. Richards was going to need to start thinking about putting her in a full-time care facility soon. He was getting pretty frail himself. I wondered what would happen to them and their properties. They had a son in another state somewhere, but I had never met him.

After they left, I settled down and decided to re-watch one of my favorite Bollywood films starring Sundar. Shortly into the movie, I fell asleep on the loveseat.

My tiny bare feet carry me down a hall. I know there is something in the room at the end — someone — I must get to. I reach the doorway and enter. He is there, on a stone slab. The old man. He is very wrinkled. His face is sunken. I go to his side, and place my tiny hand in his bony, emaciated fingers. His eyes go wide. He asks me something, and I whisper back. He smiles and breathes his last breath. He is gone. I climb on top and wail and cry. I do not want him to leave. I want him to come back. He is growing colder and stiffer, but I refuse to leave him. After a long time, someone is calling. Someone rushes in and picks me up. I scream and scream — I do not want to leave him, but I am being carried further away from him.

The sound of my own crying woke me. I looked around. The credits of the movie were rolling, and I shivered. This was not the first time for this particular nightmare, and I especially hated this one. At least my other recurring nightmare, the one where I'm searching frantically for something and suddenly falling and falling, didn't leave me with the same kind of lingering sadness, despair, and loneliness as this one always did.

Why did I have to fall asleep on the loveseat? I got up, turned off the TV, and headed into my bedroom, where my precious dreamcatcher waited to give me the peace of mind that I would have no more nightmares this evening. Even so, I cried myself back to sleep.

By the time I marched through the bitter cold and got to the office Monday morning, my temper was significantly cooled off. I was still going to have a talk with Ram about boundaries, but I imagined my tone would be much more logical and less emotional. I unlocked the door and walked through the darkened storefront to my office. I found it strange that Ram wasn't here yet. Usually, he got here bright and early. I got to work on a few projects, got caught up on my emails, and yet, there was still no Ram. Finally, Paul came in the door.

"Where's Ram?" I asked him, annoyed at myself for seeming like I might be worried about him. *I am not worried about him. Not at all.*

"Working remotely, remember? You were on the group text." Paul looked at me as guilt must've flashed over my face. "What did you do?" He gave me a mischievous smirk.

"I, uh…kinda...blocked his number?"

Paul laughed. "When I told you not to get involved, I didn't think you'd take it to the extreme, love! Perhaps you'd better unblock him, otherwise I'll never hear the end of it." He headed to his own office.

I wondered for the millionth time why Paul would put up with hearing any shit from Ram at all, still as confused as ever at this arrangement. I picked up my phone, pulled up the blocked numbers list, and removed his number. Sure enough, the group text popped up.

> Staying in the city this week. The website is live. Send me issues as they arise, and I'll fix them remotely.

There were several notifications in messages written only to me as well.

> You probably figured out what happened and blocked me. I'm sorry. I shouldn't have tracked you.

I know that you're smart and capable and wouldn't put yourself at risk. I trust you. I just needed to make sure you were ok.

You probably hate me now. I understand. I deserve it. You deserve to be surrounded by love and happiness, not deranged assholes like me.

I sat and stared at the messages for a long time. The blocking had messed with the time stamp, so I had no idea how much time had elapsed between each message. All the anger and my whole speech about boundaries I had planned went out the window. *Was he working remotely because he was ashamed to face me?*

I was glad he was up in the city. I hoped it meant he was spending some quality time with his brother and sister-in-law. Their movie was wrapping soon, and they would be heading back to India. I wondered what Ram would be doing once the website was finished. Would he go back to India as well?

I decided a reply was in order, but I wasn't sure what to write. Finally, I settled on what I hoped were the right words.

I prefer Scowling Man Bun to Deranged Asshole. It has a better ring to it. I forgive you.

After what seemed like an eternity, but was really only a few minutes, he replied.

Thank you.

P.S. It's a rishi knot, not a man bun. I have no excuse for my face.

I smiled and felt a little giddy inside. I didn't want to think about why this text exchange made me so happy.

Scowling Rishi Knot. Hmmm...it doesn't have the same impact. I think I'll have to find a new nickname for you. I'll unveil it Monday.

P.S. You're welcome.

His reply came in quickly.

Haha, I look forward to hearing it. I bet it won't be as stupid as Big Bird.

I should have been annoyed that he spied on me enough to know Zach's pet name for me, but honestly, Big Bird was a pretty stupid nickname.

Hey! How do you know about that? Your nickname is definitely going to include the word Stalker!

My phone pinged again.

I'm sorry. I have trust issues.

I sighed.

It's ok. So do I.

See you Monday, Chuli.

I knew the end of a conversation when I saw it, so I didn't reply. Instead of getting back to work, the first thing I did was go to the bookshelf of past works of Burning Wind until I found the book on Yogis and Kundalini energy, flipping through the pages until I found the section that explained proper energy-saving hair techniques performed by Yogis and Sikhs.

Ah yes, I remembered correctly. It showed a sketch of a guru looking fellow, and explained that the rishi knot is a style that is supposed to energize one's magnetic field while stimulating the pineal gland in the brain and absorbing solar energy. A wise man was always supposed to wear his hair this way during the day, and take it down to absorb lunar energy at night.

Huh. I wondered how much of this Ram believed. *If he was supposed to take it down at night, why was it still up on our date in the city?* I decided I'd ask him on Monday, now that we seemed to have reached a truce of some kind.

Until then, I determined losing myself in work was the best thing I could do. I wrote an email to every author Burning Wind represented, requesting that they look over their particular information on the site for inaccuracies and corrections and broken links.

"Here we go…" I took a deep breath and hit send, then braced myself for impact. It took about 10 minutes before the replies started rolling in and never stopped.

It truly was one of the longest work weeks I had ever experienced. The number of authors I had to soothe and hand-hold and the list of items that needed to be fixed seemed to never end, and no one seemed to be willing to wait until Monday to have it repaired. Every day, I would email a long list to Ram before leaving in the evening, and every morning, he would reply with "fixed." *Man...he's good. Does he stay up all night?* No matter what my confused feelings were on him, I was absolutely confident that he was a damn fine computer tech.

Saturday morning, I woke up refreshed after an early bedtime the night before. I chatted with Mr. Richards while my car warmed up, ready and eager to hit the gym after missing last Saturday's class. He warned me that there was a high chance of snow this afternoon, so I should hurry back as soon as my class was over, but that after the snow, the weather should be back up to normal winter temperatures. I assured him I'd be back before the first flake flew, and I headed to the gym.

Once in the locker room, I placed my belongings in an open locker. I had forgotten my padlock at home, since I was still fairly crap at the paranoid lifestyle. Ultimately I decided if someone wanted to take my clunky old phone, coat, or clothing, they were probably in worse shape than me and they could gladly have them. Besides, the Saturday morning gym people weren't exactly sketchy thief types.

I got to the class just as warm-up began and took my usual spot in the front right, furthest from the door. There were about 8 other women and one man, mostly the same people I saw every week. As I turned in a warm-up stretch, I noticed a new face in the back row. Long dark hair, hazel eyes...*could it be?* The woman made eye contact with me and smiled.

My heart was hammering in my chest, and it wasn't just because the cardio-heavy class had begun. It was the waitress from Boleto's, the one who had served me the Veruni nectar! I had gone back to the hotel to find her once I had recovered, but the staff had insisted no one that worked there fit her description. I had stalked the place several times since, and sure enough, the waitress imposter was gone. Until now.

Class couldn't seem to end fast enough. I couldn't concentrate on a single move and kept tripping over my own feet. Finally, the torture ended. I grabbed my water bottle, ready to bolt out after her while mentally planning what to say, when the instructor stopped me with a light touch on my arm.

"Hey girl, you OK? You seem like you're struggling today. Anything you want to talk about?"

It was very sweet of her, and any other time I would be touched that someone had reached out. The class was kind of clique-ish, and the instructor had never really engaged me in chit-chat before.

"Oh, thank you so much for your concern, I just have a lot going on...at work. I'll be fine."

I kindly brushed her off and headed for the locker room, hoping I hadn't missed the woman and praying I hadn't been too rude to the instructor. In the locker room, there were only two women, splashing their faces, chatting, and gathering their belongings. I hustled to the equipment room, and then the main entrance/exit at the front of the building, but she wasn't there either. *Damn it.*

All hope was not lost, though. The gym had a sign-in sheet for guests, and a machine that logged the times in and out of all members. On my way out, I would just ask the employee at the desk to look her up on the excuse that I know her from years ago, but I was too embarrassed to admit I forgot her name.

Assuring myself everything would be fine, I grabbed my towel and headed to the showers, the crown jewel of this gym, and my weekly reward for busting my butt in class. They were some kind of steamy-wonder, high-pressure hydrotherapy showers, and they were incredible.

Once I had scrubbed the sweat and grime and a little of the distress of earlier away, I dried off and headed to my locker to get changed. When I opened it, it was empty. Confused, I tried another. Did I forget which locker was mine?

I tried them all, but they were all empty, much like the locker room was. *Don't panic. Putting sweaty gym clothes back on is not the end of the world.* I went back to where I had left my gym clothes hanging next to the shower. They were gone too.

Fun-sucker and I were both getting very alarmed and scared. *Think, Chuli, breathe. One step at a time.* I tried to calm myself. *You are in a public place. You are ok. Just find some clothes. Don't they have a lost and found?* I remembered the box of lost and found items and dug through, coming up with a very tight tank top, some kind of drawstring booty pants, and a pair of flip-flops, and put them on. It wasn't much, but at least I could now get help without being completely naked.

I peered around the locker room opening to see who was left in the gym, and how to best get help. I looked in the equipment room, but it was empty. Everyone must have left early thanks to the impending snowstorm. I hugged along the wall, quietly approaching the front desk, staying out of sight, just in case. At this point, I was on high alert and not taking any chances.

I listened to two voices coming from the front desk and got close enough until I could make out what they were saying.

"What's taking so long? Can't I just go in there and knock her out? It would make it so much easier. No one is here to see."

"No, Jarred, you can't hurt her! He was very specific! He'll be very upset if you do. She probably hasn't come out yet because you went back in and stole the rest of her clothes!"

"He said to bring all her things, so I didn't want to take any chances. What if he wanted her gym clothes too?"

"I'll go get her. Then we get to see him again, and he'll be so happy with us!"

The voices seemed to belong to the front desk employee

(Jarred, apparently) and my class instructor. I remember something The Whisper had said.

"You would be a slave. You would obey every command. You would live and die with the sole purpose of pleasing your beloved."

My instincts were telling me that these two had both suffered the same chilling fate The Whisper had prevented from happening to me. I felt certain that whoever the "he" was that wanted me abducted was not anyone that I wanted to meet. I need an escape plan, fast.

I weighed my options. Could I make it to the car? *Shit. I don't have the keys.* The gym was pretty isolated, on a stretch of road with no other businesses or houses for at least a mile on either side. It wasn't a particularly well-traveled road, either. If I ran to it, the odds were pretty good that these two would catch me before I could flag down help.

About 100 yards behind the building, there was a woods line. If I ran in that direction, I could pick up a deer trail and run down to the river. Once there, I could follow it to the old rope swing. From there was a trail that led up to a much busier road where I could flag down help. I knew these woods well, and had to hope that these two didn't, so I could hopefully lose them quickly. It would be absolutely freezing, but I felt like there wasn't any other option, and I hoped I had enough adrenaline to pull it off.

"Hey!" The instructor spotted me and headed towards me.

I wasted no more time. I darted across the equipment room and slammed into the emergency side exit. An alarm went off as I opened it. A blast of arctic air slammed into me and I bolted out, heading straight for the woods. They were gaining on me, especially when I tripped over the flip-flops. I ripped them off my feet and jumped back up, ignoring the searing pain where I had scraped my knee and elbow on the pavement. I reached the woods, *yes!* and kept running, despite my fingers and toes screaming at me.

It was so cold. Their voices seemed to be far away now. *I had lost them!* Now it was time to find the river. I stopped and looked around to get my bearings. I began shivering so hard I thought my teeth might break. The sky was heavy with grey snow clouds, and the air seemed to be pressing down on me. I listened closely and heard a truck far in the distance to my left. If I just kept going straight, I should reach the river. I started walking again as quickly as I could, stumbling on numb feet. I rubbed my hands together as I walked, but I couldn't feel them either. I reached the river's edge at last.

"Ok, Chuli, you can do this!" I gave myself a clattery pep talk.

I'm looking for...something along the river, right? My brain was getting confused. *Focus Chuli! This is bad! Focus!* I finally remembered — *a rope!* I was looking for the rope swing.

The sky broke open, and billions of snowflakes poured from the sky, blanketing everything in white. They stuck to my hands, my hair, my eyelashes, everything. I lifted a hand up near my face. It was a very pretty shade of blue. I stopped for a moment to marvel at it and looked around. It was so beautiful and quiet and peaceful. I smiled and laughed. *What am I doing inside a snow globe?* Fun-sucker screamed at me to focus. Something about a rope.

I saw a bridge cross over the river very far up in the distance. Maybe I should get under there and out of the snow globe? *But it's so beautiful here, and I'm so tired. Rest first. I could share a den with a bear.* That thought made me laugh hysterically. I was no longer shivering. It was a relief.

I sat down next to a sycamore tree and closed my eyes. Something was brushing against me, nudging me. I begrudgingly opened my eyes. *Surely I am dreaming.* It was a beautiful white-tailed deer, and it kept nudging me, putting its muzzle under her arm as if to say "get up! You can't stay here!"

"Ok," I slurred, and tried my best to get up.

Who am I to argue with a deer? Somehow, I managed to get back to my feet. The doe stayed close to my side, urging me onward while keeping me upright. She seemed to be leading me somewhere, but I was too tired to pay attention. Under the bridge we went. I tried to stop to rest underneath, but the deer refused to let me until we were through the bridge and coming up on a house. I looked at it in amazement and tried to focus through the haze of my brain. I know this house. *It's Ram's house!* I recognized the greenhouses. I began to move a little faster, desperate to get to the entrance, but my feet would no longer carry me.

Crawling on my hands and knees, I managed to make it to the door. With my last bit of strength, I reached up and turned the knob. Mercifully, it opened, and I fell in, blacking out before my head hit the ground.

---

twelve

• • •

Chuli

A FAMILIAR SCENT permeated my senses when I woke up. Earthy and Divine, in equal proportions. I was laying in the dark, surrounded by soft blankets, and warm strong arms were wrapped around me. *The Whisper! How did this happen?*

"You found me," I whisper-slurred into his bare (oh my!) chest.

I was so tired, it was hard to keep awake and even harder to speak.

"No, I didn't. You found me." His chest vibrated as he spoke.

He wasn't whispering! His voice was deep and soothing, and somehow very familiar, as if I had known it this whole time.

"But...how? I don't even know your name," I got the words out, but I was still so tired. *Why was I so tired?*

"But you do, Chuli." The Whisper carefully unwound himself from me and slipped out from under the blankets.

It was dark, so I couldn't see what he was doing, but it seemed as if he had picked up something off the floor.

I was pretty sure he was putting on pants. *Was he naked*

in bed with me? Am I naked too? I tried to move my hand to do a once over to see, but my limbs felt like lead.

If we had been up to any funny business, I sure as hell didn't remember. The only things I knew were that I was very tired, very warm, and very safe, and that I was enveloped in his scent.

I closed my eyes again, breathing deep, and was almost asleep again when I felt light permeating through my closed eyelids.

"Chuli, open your eyes," He softly pleaded. *That voice again!* So soothing, so familiar.

I felt him sit on the side of the bed and I managed to get my eyes to open and focused.

Upon seeing him, the first thought I had was a memory from college. I was in a bar, and the TV was turned to the sports channel. On the screen, they were interviewing Harry Kalas, a legendary baseball sportscaster who was retiring after 40-some years. As he spoke, I had the most peculiar feeling. My dad always had the Phillies games blasting on the radio my entire childhood, and this man's voice had been the soundtrack of endless summer nights.

Seeing the man who that voice belonged to for the first time, so feeble and yet so real on the screen, had been a shock to my senses. It had taken my brain several long seconds to re-calibrate the voice to fit the body.

This was just like that, only this time, the roles were reversed. Instead of a booming voice belonging to a tiny old man, it was a soft, sweet, mostly whispering voice belonging to a hulk of a man.

His hair was down and his shirt was off, revealing a muscular chest identical to the one in my dream. But unlike my dream, Ram didn't look possessive and self-assured at all. Instead, he was looking at me with a haunted expression and an incredibly vulnerable look in his eyes, as if I could shatter him by saying the wrong thing.

Finally, I closed my eyes and said the only thing I could think of. "Like Harry, but not." And I promptly fell back to sleep.

I am in the stone hallway. My tiny bare feet carry me. I have to get to someone down the hall-the old man. He is lying on the stone. Suddenly, the wall feels hot. I look over and pull my hand away, but it is too late. The wall is angry, red and pulsing, and it has burned me. I look down. The heat has spread to the floor, and is now burning my feet. I try to run to the old man, but the intense heat is spreading up my limbs. I scream in agony. I am being burned alive.

---

thirteen

. . .

Ram

I TRIED to comfort Chuli while doing my best to keep calm. She was screaming in agony and thrashing about, either having a nightmare or delusional with pain, or perhaps both. She was getting tangled in the covers.

I turned the light on and pulled the covers back and gently held her in place by her shoulders while continuing to call to her. Finally, I seemed to break through and she opened wide, terrified eyes. "Fire...I'm on fire..." She choked out between sobs.

I put some space between us to examine her in the light. The danger of hypothermia had passed, but now she was burning up. Her arms and legs suffered from a number of cuts and scrapes, but her hands and feet looked awful. They were severely frostbitten, and had turned a splotchy, swollen red. Blisters were forming, some blood-filled. Parts of them were varying shades of purple. Her nose and ears were beginning to suffer the same fate.

She continued crying and thrashing, incoherent with pain. I couldn't stand to watch any longer. I had to do something to help her, and quickly. I got up, ran to my bag, and pulled out the standard-issue High Order emergency medicine kit. I hesitated for a brief moment. The contents were strictly regulated by the High Order and were not to be given to an unauthorized subject. There would definitely be consequences later, as the High Order didn't take kindly to any rule-breaking, but as Chuli cried, I decided she was worth whatever punishment they'd dish out to me later.

I opened the kit and found the little bottle with the dropper I was looking for. The medicine was extremely potent and tasted terrible. Normally, I would dilute it with something else, but I didn't want to waste any more time. I brought it back to the bed and tried to hold her still.

"Open your mouth, love," I said, but she couldn't hear me, so I cradled her head back and squirted some drops in her mouth.

Immediately, she began to gag. She sat up and doubled over as she coughed and wretched. She cleared her throat a final time and then went still and quiet. I used the tips of my fingers to gently brush her sweat-soaked hair out of her face and behind her shoulder.

"Better?"

She slowly nodded while taking a deep breath. Her fever was already beginning to cool, and clearly the pain was improving greatly. The medicine began circulating in her system, healing everything in its path.

"I'll go put the kettle on for some tea. It's important that you stay hydrated. I'll run a bath as well. I imagine you'll want to get cleaned up."

She nodded but didn't say anything. She was marveling at the way the blisters and cuts were vanishing before her eyes, leaving dried blood and fluid in their wake. It was truly magic, and impressive to watch.

I got up, turned on the kettle in the kitchen, and went to the bathroom to turn on the tub faucet. I sat on the edge of the garden tub, watching the dawn light begin to creep through the window. It was the first time I had left her side since she showed up late yesterday morning, slumping over the threshold, blue and snow-covered, wearing only a tank top and short shorts. I still had no idea what had happened to her and how she had found me, but I sent a prayer of thanks out to anyone Upstairs or in the High Order that might have had anything to do with it.

Her pulse was so weak and slow, and she felt like a solid block of ice as I gently carried her to the bed and cut the wet clothes off her. I had removed my own clothes and climbed in next to her, knowing that skin-to-skin contact was still the safest, most tried and true method of warming someone. It felt like it took forever for her body to warm, and her breathing and heart rate to return to normal.

During that time, I promised myself that if she survived, I would no longer hide the details of what was happening. She deserved to know the truth about everything. I had almost lost my nerve when she had finally and briefly woken up. She had sighed so contentedly against my chest when she believed I had somehow found her.

She still hadn't made the connection that her whispering hero in the dark was also her co-worker, and I was afraid of what her reaction would be once she found out I was no hero at all — just a jaded, scowling jerk with stupid hair. Clearly she had a temper. She'd blocked me on her phone after one little infraction and had half-jokingly called me a stalker. If she knew the full extent of it, she may just block me forever.

Unfortunately, I knew coming clean and facing the consequences was the only way to end this stalemate, and it was a risk I needed to take. I cared about her too much to continue this secrecy. I had held her for one last moment knowing it could potentially be the last, and tried to memorize the feel of her against my body, and how it was a perfect fit. I unwound myself from her, got up, and turned the light on, readying myself for the shock and anger that was sure to come.

Instead, her reaction was baffling. She didn't seem the slightest bit mad, or even surprised. Had she actually known? And why was her only response something about a guy named Harry? I wondered if maybe she was delusional, and still didn't understand, so the fear of rejection hadn't entirely subsided yet.

After her tea and bath, we were going to talk about a whole lot of things. I knew she was strong. New Years and whatever happened yesterday had taught me that. But she was about to go through a whole other round of mental turmoil. I prayed she could handle it, all while having deep faith in her that she could.

---

fourteen

• • •

Chuli

MY BATH HELPED CLEAR my head a bit. I was still in pain, but it was nothing like the intense agony I had experienced earlier this morning. I examined my now clean feet as they stuck out above the soapy water. They were pink, with faint scars where the blisters had been. Normally, frostbite was something that took months to heal. Clearly, whatever Ram had given me was not from this world. But that made sense, now that he had revealed he was actually The Whisper, and therefore also not of this world.

I supposed I should be furious with him for not telling me the truth from the beginning. I felt like a total idiot for not knowing. We'd been working side by side for months now. Perhaps that was why he always maintained a polite distance and was always so clipped in his speech? Maybe he didn't want me to know. *Know what?* I still didn't know who or what he was.

Given my recent brush with death, and that fact that someone was apparently trying very hard to abduct me, I decided right then and there to let go of any anger towards him. I was certain he was trying to protect me, and I needed all the help I could get right now. I emerged from the tub and put on the clothes Ram had laid out for me: T-shirt, soft drawstring pants, and a robe, all way too big.

As I adjusted the tee-shirt in the mirror, I remembered adjusting my own shirt in the mirror on Valentine's Day after...I made out with Ram, and it had been the best kiss of my entire life. I felt my cheeks warm. *Damn it, even my subconscious had known and dreamt about him!* I couldn't think about that now, as there were more pressing matters at hand. I closed my eyes for a moment and set an intention to go into whatever conversation we were about to have with an open mind. Then I slipped my feet into soft, too-big slippers, and shuffled out to the living room.

Ram sat on one end of the sofa. He had cups of tea waiting for both of us. *Damn, a girl could get used to that,* I thought, as I sat down sideways on the other end, facing him, ignoring my body's urge to snuggle up next to him.

"You look much better. How do you feel?" He asked, looking truly concerned. He had truly been a wonderful caretaker so far.

"Ok, considering. It still hurts, but not...like before." I shuddered to think of how intense that throbbing pain had been.

We sat in silence for a moment. There was so much to talk about, but it was difficult to know where to start. Finally, Ram began.

"I want to tell you everything, and I will, I promise. But first, please, Chuli," he leaned forward and took my hand, as if he felt that same urge to connect our bodies in some way. "Tell me, what happened to you? How did you get here, and why were you..." his voice went soft with emotion, as if it pained him to recall, "...frozen...like that?"

I thought about what I must have looked like. It was probably a terrifying sight to behold no matter who the person was, if they were blue and covered in snow and collapsed in a doorway.

"I was at the gym. The waitress was there, the one from Boleto's. She was in my class. I tried to catch up with her, but the instructor held me back...oh, now I see. That was on purpose!"

Ram tried to follow. "You saw the waitress?"

"Yes! But I couldn't get to her in time. I was going to ask the front desk for her name when I left, but then everyone was gone, and the front desk employee stole my clothes..."

"Why?" Ram looked ready to murder Jarred.

"I don't know! I heard them talking, the front desk employee, and the instructor. They said they were to gather all of my stuff and 'bring me to him'. Ram — I think they were given the nectar. I don't think they were thinking straight at all."

Ram closed his eyes. "Damn it. Two more! Right under my nose." He was clearly upset. "I'm sorry, I shouldn't have interrupted. Please continue."

I looked at him. *How had I thought he was arrogant?* I was continuing to merge the two identities of Ram and The Whisper into one person, clicking pieces together and getting a more rounded view of a complex person/whatever he was. It was now obvious to me that Ram always put others before himself. I resisted the urge to comfort him and continued.

"I grabbed whatever I could from the lost and found, and ran out the emergency exit and into the woods. It was my only hope of losing them. I followed a deer trail down to the river. I was going to take the rope swing path up to the turnpike bridge to flag down help, but...it was so cold. I got confused. I think...I think I forgot what I was doing." I pondered for a moment, trying to remember. "I remember thinking I was in a snow globe, and sitting down next to a sycamore tree. And then..." I gasped, remembering the deer.

I jumped off the couch and went to the door, concern

flooding my body. *Was she still out there, waiting to see if I was ok? Did I imagine the whole thing?* I needed to return to the woods line to see for myself. Ram didn't try to stop me. He followed behind as I trudged out into the morning light.

About 4 inches of snow had fallen. I kept walking until I reached the woods and tuned into my senses. It seemed easier to do somehow, and I wondered if it was from whatever magic medicine Ram gave me. Within moments, I spotted her. *The deer was real!* She was standing between two hemlocks. I smiled and walked towards her.

When I reached her, I dropped to my knees in the snow, bowed my head, and said, "You saved my life. Thank you, thank you, thank you!"

The deer nuzzled against my shoulder and I wrapped my arms around her and hugged her, tearing up. I let go and the doe took a few steps back to look at me.

"She says you're welcome, little Brown Bird of Bear Mountain. She is glad you're OK." Ram said as he came up next to me and gave me a hand getting back on my feet.

"You can talk to her?" I asked him in awe.

He nodded.

"How do you know me?" I asked the deer.

She looked at me, and then at Ram. "She says the whole forest knows you. Your father...asked the Great Spirit to protect you and keep you safe in these woods. The Great Spirit will honor those wishes."

I didn't know what to say. I had spent my childhood running around in these woods and had never once felt like I was in danger. Now I supposed I knew why. The cold snow was beginning to sting where it had gotten in my slippers and soaked the knees of my pants.

"Now she says I had better get you back inside before you freeze again." He pressed his palms together in a prayer formation and bowed to the deer.

The doe dipped her head, turned, and walked away. I

stood for a moment, watching her leave, and then turned to go back inside.

"Let me help you," Ram said as he picked me up and put me in his arms. I wanted to protest, but it felt really nice, so I wrapped my arms around his neck.

"How can you talk to deer?" I asked him.

"Let's get back inside first. There's a whole lot more we need to talk about."

Once I was nestled back under the covers in Ram's bed, my wet pants hanging to dry, Ram placed my slippers by the heater and sat down on the edge to join me. I was sitting upright, my back leaning against the soft headboard. Ram really did have quite a nice bed.

"Here, come sit where you can relax. You look exhausted," I patted the bed next to me.

He obliged, but he stayed on top of the covers. As soon as he was settled, I began. "Let's start with the basics. Who, or...what, are you? You already told me you're not human, but you look pretty damn human to me. So what gives?"

He turned toward me and leaned the side of his head against the headboard. It seemed like he was trying to determine where to begin. Finally, he spoke.

"I am what they call one of the Old Gods. I am not from here, but this body, my current form, is biologically human."

He paused and looked at my face. Perhaps he was searching for denial, or anger, or accusations that he was nuts. He wasn't going to find any of those, though.

"And…" I encouraged him to keep going.

"And in this life, I am also an officer of the High Order. It's kind of like the FBI, but we monitor the earth for any...celestial infidelities. Earth rules are pretty straightforward. No killing, no revealing ourselves to humans, and absolutely no using any sacred elixirs, drugs, potions or herbs from our world on humans."

He paused, but I still didn't have any questions for him, so he continued. "I received a tip that a Forgotten had gotten a hold of some Veruni nectar. We chased the lead near here before the trail went cold. The High Order made an arrangement with Paul to place me undercover in his publishing company, but Paul insisted the only way he was going to allow it was if I built you a website."

"Wait...you're not really a computer tech!?"

Ram began laughing. It was a beautiful sight and sound.

"I tell you I'm a god and a secret agent, and you witnessed me talking to a deer, and the only part that seems to concern you is that I'm not really a computer tech?" He started bellowing with laughter again.

It seemed to be contagious, and I started laughing too. "Well, when you put it that way, I guess that is a pretty weird concern. But you're just so...good at it, I assumed you've built hundreds of websites before."

He smiled at me. "I'm flattered that you think so. I actually enjoyed that part quite a bit more than I thought I would. I've really only made one other website, and it's more of a database, really."

The more he talked, the lighter and friendlier he seemed to become. I wondered if it was because he finally had the ability to be himself in front of me.

"OK, question time. Can you talk to all animals? And what god are you? And where do you come from? How do you get to Earth? Are you immortal?"

"Whoa...slow down there. One at a time. Yes, I can communicate with animals. Where I come from is a very large and varied place. There are several ways to get down to Earth. I usually take the direct jump method, although sometimes I put in a request if I want something specific. This time around, I requested a body and name closely aligned to my usual form Upstairs."

"So what are you the god of?"

"I'm the god of many things, especially agriculture and strength. Usually, my most legendary role is that of big brother."

"You're...oh my...you're Balarama, aren't you?" I sat in awe as he nodded his head.

I thought back to that first night, when he was helping me get through the Veruni nectar. Of all the gods I had to rip on, I had ranted about Balarama. *I had called him a pompous douche to his face!* I cringed in shame when I realized I'd asked him if his wife had cared about his cheating ways. His wife, whom I now knew, killed herself. *No wonder he couldn't stand the sight of me.*

"Ram...I mean...Lord Balarama.."

"Ram is fine," he said.

"Oh...it's not fine. I…"

He smiled, but that smile was now tinged with sadness. "Called me a pompous douche? It's OK. It's the truth."

I really wasn't sure what to do or say. Here I was, in bed with a god. A god whom I had gravely insulted, yet who seemed to care about my safety regardless. I did the only thing I could think of. I wrapped my arms around him and gave him a hug.

"I'm so sorry," I whispered.

He was tense at first, but eventually he gave in and let me comfort him. We stayed like that for several long moments until the air changed, as if we both remembered the kiss we shared, and my body became aware of every place his body touched mine. My breathing became a little shallow, and I could hear his heartbeat pick up as well.

BOOM! BOOM!

There was an angry pounding at the door. I pulled back, alarmed, ready to make a break for it again if I needed to.

Ram jumped out of bed. "That would be Paul. I told him you were here. I'll go let him in before he breaks my door."

I got out of bed and put my pants back on. They were

still a little damp, but they weren't too bad. I headed towards the living room.

Paul and Stewie were just coming in the door, and Paul was yelling at Ram. "...destroy everything she has? So what, you can just steal her now, asshole? High Order be damned, you can't just take her away!"

"Hey, whoa...Ram's not taking me anywhere! He saved me, Paul. Why are you so upset? I mean I know you told me not to get involved with him, but…"

I was interrupted by crushing hugs on both sides from Paul and Stewie. "Goddess, you're still alive! How are you here!?" Paul exclaimed through tears.

I was definitely weirded out. "Paul, I'm sorry if Ram's message scared you. I don't know what all you know about the gym yesterday, but I can assure you, I'll be fine. I've still got some pain from the frostbite, but.."

"Frostbite? What the fuck, woman! How did you get frostbite in a fire!?"

"Fire? Who said anything about a fire?" I was deeply confused.

"You didn't tell her?" Paul looked at Ram, outraged. Ram just looked at him with a puzzled look on his face, as if he wasn't sure how to answer, so I did.

"Tell me what? That he's a god that works for the High Order that talks to deer? He did tell me."

"You can talk to deer?" It was Stewie who spoke, quietly observing from my side. He looked intrigued. "Cool," he said to no one in particular.

"Wait...you two are gods as well!" I was beginning to put the pieces together.

Stewie smiled at me. Paul retreated from his aggressive stance towards Ram and came back over to me. "Yes, sweets, and we can talk about that later. Right now, there's something you need to know."

I didn't like the feeling I was getting and I braced myself for very bad news.

"Yesterday...you...died. In a fire."

I was very confused as I looked around at the three men — gods — surrounding me. They all had varying degrees of pity etched on their faces, though Ram looked surprised and confused, as if this was the first he was hearing about it as well.

I took a step back, as if to distance myself from whatever further news Paul was about to share, but he caught my hand. I felt a surge of relaxation creep up my arm. Now that I knew he was a god and had special powers, I thought about how touching him had always made me feel better, and I assumed this was one of his unique powers. I pulled my hand back.

"Don't do that. I don't want comfort. I want the truth."

Paul looked surprised, but like he respected my decision, so he began to explain. "Yesterday, there was an explosion and a fire at your house,"

I interrupted him, my voice rising in panic. "What?! How? Please tell me the Richards are OK!"

"They're ok. Mr. Richards suffered some smoke inhalation and a few mild burns trying to get to you, but he is expected to recover. He is currently being treated at the hospital."

"But why was he trying to get to me? I wasn't home. He saw me leave," I crossed and uncrossed my arms with nervous energy.

Paul lowered his voice to just above a whisper. "But Chuli, you were home. He saw you pull up in your car and run inside. You even waved at him on your way in. Moments later, he said he heard your blender turn on, and then an explosion. He ran over, but the flames were already too hot. By the time I got there, the fire company had the blaze under control. Chuli…" Paul's voice cracked and tears swelled in his eyes, "They pulled your body out of the rubble. I saw them...put you in a body bag and take you away."

Now it was Stewie's turn to offer comfort. He wrapped his arms around his husband. I had never seen Paul cry about anything ever, yet here he was, crying as he recalled what must have been a horrifying scene. I didn't know what to do or say. None of this made sense. My brain reeled, and then something clicked into place.

I looked at Ram. "The waitress looked like me," I said to him.

He paused, then closed his eyes and nodded his head in acknowledgment. I explained to Paul and Stewie what had happened to me at the gym and my theory about the waitress. My guess was that she had dressed in my stolen clothing with my coat, my phone, and keys, stolen my car, and pretended to be me, and then somehow killed herself in an explosion at my house, most likely on the orders of whomever had the Veruni Nectar.

"Whoever this piece of shit is wanted the world to think you were dead," Paul concluded.

I calmly excused myself and went to the bathroom, where I promptly emptied the contents of my stomach into the toilet. *That waitress died for me. Those gym workers stole and attempted kidnapping because of me. Mr. Richards was injured and nearly killed because of me.* And now the world thought I was dead, and all of my belongings had gone up in flames.

I wretched into the toilet until there was nothing left, and then crumpled onto the floor, leaning against the tub, eyes closed. Ram quietly entered and sat down next to me. He wrapped his arm around me, and nestled my head so it was more comfortable against the front of his shoulder. He tenderly stroked my hair with his other hand. Ram knew there was nothing he could say to make me feel better, so he didn't try.

After a few minutes, I found the outlet I needed. Tears. I cried and sobbed and cried some more. When I had no more tears left to cry, Ram disentangled himself from me and helped me up.

"Come on, I want to show you something." He held my hand and gently tugged me along, out of the bathroom, and back through the living room, where Paul and Stewie patiently waited on the sofa.

I followed him out the back patio doors, across the covered veranda to the greenhouse door. When we entered, the first thing that hit me was the fragrance. Petrichor — earth after rain. One of my favorite words and one of my favorite smells, and it lingered in the air. This was the earthy part of Ram's unique scent. Earth and rain mixed with the heady scents of flowers, herbs, and vegetables. It smelled of life, of spring, of hope.

Ram walked me through the incredible greenhouse, bursting at the seams with all manner of plants, pointing out different varieties. He really was the god of agriculture. No mortal could keep a greenhouse like this. It was hard to stay in a state of despair while taking it all in.

When we reached the end of the rows, we came to a beautiful area that looked almost like a small courtyard, complete with a fountain. Ram turned to me and placed his hands gently on my shoulders. He looked me in the eyes.

"Chuli, this is not your fault. You have no reason to feel guilty. You did nothing wrong. You didn't hurt those people. If it's anyone's fault, it's my own." Ram removed his hands from my shoulders. "I'm the agent on this case, but I've been so self-absorbed that I've allowed three more people to get poisoned, right under my nose. That poor waitress lost her life because of me."

He looked incredibly distraught and angry with himself as he turned away from me.

"Hey, " I said as I reached out to switch to the role of comforter, "This isn't your fault either! It's the scumbag poisoner's fault. We need to try to figure out who the hell he is, so we can bring him down."

"I've been trying, but every lead I get turns up cold! We've already exhausted your list of potential enemies or bitter exes. Your brother is an asshole, but has no connections to our world..."

"You suspected my brother?" I became nauseous at the thought of my brother slipping me love potion.

"He had to be ruled out, but it wasn't him," He assured me, noting the look of horror on my face.

He continued. "My only real suspect was that douchebag author with the stupid nickname for you."

Now Ram was the one who looked nauseous. I almost became defensive of Zach, but now that I knew he wasn't The Whisper, all romantic feelings towards him vanished. *Now I know The Whisper is right here with me. Do I have romantic feelings for him?* The thought entered my head, but I angrily told myself and Fun-sucker (who seemed to be screaming *yes you do!!!)* to shut up, that now was not the time to think about such trivial things.

"I've been tracking him in the city all week. Besides learning he's a disgusting piece of shit who frequents hook-up apps, he seems to be innocent. All follow-ups with his dates revealed no traces of Veruni or any of its effects."

"Follow-ups, eh, Ram?" Teased Paul, who had just arrived in the greenhouse with a very awestruck Stewie. "You swiped right on all his sloppy seconds?" He laughed.

In a flash, Ram's fist connected with Paul's face, which made a horrible crunching sound.

"Hey!" Paul yelled, holding his hand up to his nose,"

That wasn't very nice!" He removed his hand, revealing a trickle of blood from his nose. He was glaring at Ram.

I watched in horror, frozen in place, as Ram gripped his own neck and fell to his knees, as if he could no longer breathe. I was just about to spring into action to try to help him, when suddenly the pressure eased and Ram gasped for air.

I looked at Paul, who casually wiped the last of the blood from his nose with a handkerchief, showing no outward signs of injury.

He walked over and offered his hand to Ram as he said, "Let's think before we swing next time, yes?"

Ram looked up at him and respectfully nodded. He took his offered hand and was back on his feet.

"Although I do suppose my comment was a little out of line, so we'll call it even," Paul nodded as if he had just decided it and now it was so, which I supposed it was.

"He is not interested in that. He's…pure" Stewie's quiet but resonant voice spoke as he peered at Ram and then the ring on Ram's finger, with a fascinated look on his face.

I wondered what pure meant, but I was dealing with so many things at this moment that my brain had given up on trying to find reason.

"This brute? A virgin? Ha! That explains so much!" Paul burst out laughing.

Ram appeared ready to hit him again, but instead, he kept quiet as he touched his neck, remembering the consequences of his last rash action.

My brain had now absorbed so much information that it was heading into shut-down mode. My eyes began closing on their own, and I was pretty sure I was going to fall over if I stood here any longer.

"I'm..." I struggled to get the words out to explain my predicament, but it turned out I didn't need any.

Ram picked me up again, just as he had this morning.

As he carried me back inside to his bed, he spoke. "You need rest. They will stay with you and keep you safe. I have to report this to the High Order and see if I can pick up any further trace. I will be back as soon as I know anything."

With that, he gently deposited me back in bed, adjusted the covers, and kissed the top of my head as I closed my eyes and drifted off.

---

fifteen

. . .

Chuli

AFTER MY NAP, Paul and Stewie took me and a big basket of produce courtesy of Ram's greenhouse back to the Chateau for better protection. The ride home was heavy. I had begged them to drive by my house. I needed to see it to fully believe the enormity of what happened there.

Through the car window, I could see that my house was a burned-out shell. The windows had all blown out, and I could see a soggy, burned mess of everything I owned inside. I longed to go in and see if there was something, anything at all I could salvage, but Paul refused to stop the car. He insisted that until the mastermind behind this was apprehended, it wasn't safe for me to let anyone know I was still alive.

Something bright caught my eye on the steps to the front door. It was a bundle of yellow tulips. I was sure they were from Lucy, the only person besides Paul that knew yellow tulips were my favorite. *Lucy thought I was dead. If I could tell her the truth, would she even believe me? How will I go about salvaging my life when this is over?*

Once we were safely inside the Chateau, Stewie left to pick up a few outfits for me. Paul insisted I needed food, and got me a banana and some peanut butter toast before we sat in the stools at the island counter.

"Idun's extract can only go so far. It's important that you give your body some calories and protein. It will help you heal faster."

"Idun's. Is that what Ram gave me to heal the frostbite?" I asked between bites.

"Indeed. The very same stuff you've been using on your face since you got back from the city — don't think I didn't notice. The beauty bottle form is a very diluted version, however. Nice for a little boost, but it doesn't have nearly the healing properties to tackle something as severe as bringing you back from the verge of death like that."

"Idun's the Norse goddess with the magic apples that keep the gods young, right? She's real?" I wondered.

"She is, or so I hear. I've never actually met her. She's kind of like the Madame C.J. Walker of the Upstairs. She figured out a way to make her fruits go even further by extracting them, and she makes a fortune selling various beauty products. The extract that you had, however, is a High Order exclusive. It's military-grade, for agent use only in extreme situations. Highly illegal for anyone else, immortal god or not."

"Is that how you get your powers?"

Even though I was weak, my body felt enhanced somehow. If a human like me felt that way, perhaps it had an even more pronounced effect on gods.

"No. Our powers are tied to our faith."

"How do you mean?"

"Each god's powers are unique. Generally, they are a very private thing we don't share with other gods. The strength of those powers is directly tied to how many humans believe in us. I, like Ram, am one of the Old Gods. That means we are some of the earliest and strongest gods, only because we've been around the longest and our names are still commonly known throughout humankind."

"What Old God are you, Paul?"

"Guess," Paul asked with a smile.

I thought about everything I knew about him. He loved the arts: literature, music, dancing. Although he had been in America for a long time, I knew he was born in Greece.

"Phoebus Apollo?" I guessed.

"Damn, Chuli, you're good! But drop the Phoebus. That ship set sail a looooong time ago."

I was fascinated, but figured I could get some stories another time. "What about Stewie? Is he an Old God?"

"Stewie's life and stories are not mine to tell. Perhaps he will tell you on his own one day. For now, let's go back to the types of gods. There are us Old Gods, but then, on the other end of the spectrum, are the Forgottens. They are the gods whom no one remembers. Because of that, their powers are dwindling. They come down to Earth to try to make their mark, to see if someone might remember them."

Something clicked inside. "That's why you founded Burning Wind Press! You wanted to give the Forgottens a chance to get some strength back!"

I smiled at him, and he smiled back with a nod. "I'm an equal opportunity immortal."

"Back to the Idun extract. Does it keep you immortal while here on Earth? Can you just stay here as long as you want?"

"No. Our earthly shells are mortal. It helps us look nice, and can heal us if we are very sick or badly injured, but it cannot prevent our death or entirely prevent us from aging."

"So you're not immortal?"

"We are. It's our souls that are immortal, however." Paul scooted in his chair. "I should probably explain how souls work, Chuli. Usually, when humans die, their souls wind up in a sort of...endless recycling program. They get sent to...somewhere I've never been, so I'm not sure exactly how it works, but somehow they get wiped clean, and put back down into another human body, ready for reuse."

"So there is no Heaven or Hell for humans?" I finished my toast and began peeling my banana. Paul was right about the food. I was already feeling a bit more energetic.

"Well...I've heard rumors that both really do exist for the devout and the cruel, but honestly, I'm not really sure how it works everywhere. The Upstairs is a very big place, with lots of mysterious things going on. It's every sacred god or spirit that ever existed. There's plenty of areas where even I have never been, though I have heard tales that the pearly gates are real."

I pondered this for a moment. "What happens to gods' souls when they die? Do you just go back to the Upstairs?"

"You're right, that's exactly what happens. Our souls depart and are received at one of the many portals Upstairs. They are kind of like airports, or train stations, with a rigorous customs protocol. The High Order officers interrogate us, the sanctimonious pricks that they are, and look for wanted criminals and contraband. The portals have a way of suspending all powers, and some of those douches really lord it over us, knowing we can't do anything about it."

"Is that why you hate Ram? Because he's from the High Order?" I concluded that had to be why. If Paul had nothing but bad experiences with the High Order, he would naturally bristle at an agent.

"So astute! Yes indeed. Those High Order bastards are all the same. Self-inflated Forgottens who have nothing better to do than follow orders and hunt down gods looking to have a little fun."

"Fun? Like drugging, kidnapping, and murdering people?" My voice held a note of anger.

Paul had the decency to look ashamed. "Chuli, love, no.

I suppose they do have a purpose, I had just never really considered it before. And Ram...well maybe he's not so bad. He's still an asshole, but perhaps hate is too strong a word. Clearly he cares very much for you. But once this is done, he'll just get reassigned elsewhere and vanish from your life. That's why I wanted you to stay away from him. I'd hate to see you get hurt."

I looked at the faint pink scars on my hands and feet and laughed. "A little late for that!"

"That's not what I mean. I don't want to see you get hurt any which way, but physical wounds can heal. There is no Idun's Extract for heartbreak, however."

I didn't want to talk about any budding feelings between me and Ram, and I didn't want to think about what would happen when this was all over, so I steered the conversation back to safer territory.

"Ram said he usually jumps down to Earth. Is that how you got here too?"

"Good heavens, I am not a jumper! When I decide to visit Earth, I plan my journey thoroughly, including requesting very specific things. I depart through the portals, like any other civilized god would. To just jump like that is...crazy. You'd get to the same place — all gods are born wherever their soul originated from — but you'd have no control over what kind of life you'd lead. You'd have to be in quite a rush to get back down. Why you would want to is beyond me."

I thought of Ram again, and how he said he usually jumped except for this time. Usually connotes many trips to Earth. I didn't know how many he had taken and why he usually chose that particular route. Then I thought of his wife, jumping from the cliff. *Lost*, Radha had called her. "What's a Lost? Is that when a god's soul dies?"

Paul studied me for a long moment, as if he was deciding how much to tell me. "There are very few ways a god's soul can die. There used to be demons that had those abilities, but they were all rooted out and destroyed eons ago. So now, if an immortal has decided they've truly had enough, there is only one route left. Becoming Lost."

"How does it work?"

"Well, the first thing you have to do is find a wortcunner."

I knew from my years at Burning Wind that a wortcunner was a woman, *probably a goddess*, I thought with my newfound knowledge, who worked with herbal healing and magic.

"Then, you have to get a specific magic herb bundle from her. Once you have it, you brew it into a strong tea in a very specific way. Then you drink it, stand on the edge of the Bluff, and call out an incantation several times. After that, you...jump."

"What happens then?"

"Then, you are bound to Earth. When you die, your soul goes to the same place as the humans, and gets wiped clean and recycled, but that's all we really know. There's really only been a push in the past few years to learn more about them, and potentially save them. We've learned that they are still like the gods in that they are born in their original birthplace, which could help tremendously with returning them to their loved ones for identification. A database was begun to help track them, to help their loved ones find them again, but I have no idea what happens once you are identified."

I thought of Ram and how he had mentioned using his computer skills to build a database. I was pretty sure I knew exactly why Ram kept returning to Earth. *He was trying to find his wife and bring her home again.* Then something Paul said stopped me.

"What do you mean, 'you'?"

"What?"

"You said, 'I don't know what happens once you are identified'. Why did you say that?"

Paul touched my arm. This time, I let his soothing comfort wash over me. I suspected I was going to need it for whatever Paul said next, and I was right.

"Chuli, my Goddess..." Paul began, but there was no need to say it. I was *Lost.* I began to laugh, a maddening sort of cackle. It was the only response left.

I stood in the bathroom and looked at myself in the mirror as I braided my long wet hair. I had showered and changed into the lovely soft pajamas Stewie had so thoughtfully picked out for me, and I tried to make out the "spotty, erratic aura" that Paul claimed the Lost possessed, but I wasn't having much luck.

Physically, I was feeling much better, thanks to an expertly prepared dinner Stewie had fashioned over his prizes from Ram's greenhouse. Mentally, however, my head was spinning. I had learned so very much in the past few days. My life as I knew it was gone, along with everything I owned. Gods were real. So was the person trying to kidnap and drug me.

To top it off, apparently I had a suicidal god trapped inside me. I was Lost — *a Lost?* — I, Chuli Davis, editor of perhaps hundreds of books, didn't even know the correct words to use to describe myself.

But through all this turmoil and uncertainty, some parts of my life so far became clearer somehow. *This was why many of the authors I worked with and many of Paul's friends viewed me with varying degrees of curiosity and pity. This was why Paul had thrown me that birthday party.*

Three years ago, I had no one to celebrate my 25th birthday with. My mom had recently departed for the monastery and had taken her vow of silence, and my dad was no longer living. Paul invited me over to the Chateau and surprised me with a full-on Pow-Wow. There was a sweat lodge, a big campfire, songs, and dances.

Everyone there was Native American and dressed in full tribal regalia. No one spoke English or even Lenape, which I really only knew a few words of, but it didn't make it any less special. Paul had even managed to bring the dreamcatcher my Dad made me that always hung above my bed — he must've worked something out with my landlord, Mr. Richards — and they performed several ceremonies around it. Paul said that since I'd had so many bad dreams as a child, it was important that they remove them for me so it could continue protecting me.

I was in awe that he could know so much about me. *How did he know I had so many nightmares?* That act cemented him into a special place in my heart forever, even though I couldn't communicate with anyone there but him and Stewie. But now I knew there was something else going on that night. All those Native Americans looking at me with concern — they were trying to recognize me, but apparently none of them had. He was trying to help me find my family.

I may not know which god lived inside me, but I was, however, determined not to completely lose my shit. I had fought off the Veruni nectar, something that had waylaid a powerful god for a month, maybe longer, in a single night. Granted, I had help, but I had to believe in myself. I could get through this. Sometimes, moments of great pain create great clarity. I decided the best chance I had at sorting out this mess was to lean into it.

I sat cross-legged on the plush carpet in the guest room, ready to meditate, a practice I'd been working on for years. It was the very same room I had slept in on Valentine's Day. The night that The Whisp...Ram kissed me. I figured I had better start with that tangle of thoughts.

I closed my eyes and visualized a ball of energy. I suspected the Idun's extract would help bring another dimension to my meditation practice, and I was right. The energy ball was in vivid detail, a tangled mess of colored ropes. I pictured each colored rope as a specific train of thought.

I picked out the crimson one, the one that represented my feelings towards Ram. When I had met him, I had thought him arrogant, jaded, rude, and obnoxious. Learning about his wife's suicide, I had understood that this was a mask he wore to hide the guilt, shame, pain, and grief hiding within. But he had kissed me senseless, which showed me that there was still plenty of love and passion within him. I delved deeper into myself, to examine my own feelings towards him. I realized I cared quite a bit for him. I wanted to bring him comfort and happiness, to make his face light up in that glorious smile. But he still longed for his wife.

For a moment, I considered that perhaps I was his lost wife, but the facts didn't add up. First of all, he certainly would have said something to me about it. *Wouldn't he?* Even if he didn't, Paul had explained that all gods, including the Lost, are born in their ancestral homeland. I was born here, in America. I was certain Revati, his wife, had to have come from India or some other nearby country in Asia, so I ruled myself out. *Could I, another Lost, make him forget his wife in time?* That thought made me sad. I didn't want to be an interloper on his marriage.

Stewie claimed he was a virgin. *How did Stewie know that anyway? Is that one of his powers? Knowing people's sexual history? Weird.* Ram was faithful to her. He was probably feeling awful about our kiss. He definitely seemed to care about me, but how much of that was because I was Lost, like her? Did he believe if he could save me, then there was still hope left for Revati? *But why hadn't he told me I was Lost?* Perhaps he was planning on it, but wasn't sure how to broach the subject. It was a pretty awkward thing to tell someone, and we got interrupted pretty soon after I recovered from my attempted abduction.

I acknowledged my feelings as I focused on the tangled crimson rope: Care, compassion, perhaps even a little jealousy towards his wife. I gave them each a silent nod, and allowed the crimson rope to untangle and float away.

Next up, the blue rope. This one was the sadness and grief. My belongings, especially the ones that used to belong to my father, my friendships with Lucy and Mr. Richards, the senseless life taken from the waitress. I let a few tears fall. I would be kind to myself. It was OK to feel sadness and anger. But staying in that feeling too long could only harm me. There was no going backward in time to fix these things, so it was OK to set these feelings down for a while so I could function. The blue rope uncoiled itself and floated away.

Next, wrapped and bound tightly against the core of the ball was an angry, writhing rope. Alternating with red and black, it reminded me of a smoldering fire. This one represented one of the most urgent matters. Someone was after me. He had drugged me, made the world think I was dead, burned down my house, and killed people in his quest to get me. He was still out there, and I had no idea how to find him.

I leaned into the feelings and validated them: fear, anxiety, anger, and pain. All justifiable. *But did they help to actually catch him? Did they keep me safe?* Not at the moment.

At the moment, I was safely tucked inside the home of two gods, one strong enough to choke other gods with a glare. Another powerful god was out in the world, with the High Order on his side, trying to get to the bottom of all this. I was living the paranormal equivalent of a military level security detail of a high ranking official.

I promised these very strong feelings that they too would be allowed back later, when I was in need of them, but they had to leave right now. I watched them reluctantly unwind and slowly fade away from the ball in my mind.

Now, there was only the core remaining. It was a shimmering, golden orb. If I could penetrate it, I felt certain it would contain the answers to the current situation. *Who was inside that orb? Was the Veruni actually meant for them? How could I break through this barrier in my mind?* I let my mind wander freely, putting out feelers for any answers. Suddenly, I had a thought. *My nightmares! What if they were actually repressed memories breaking through?*

I had lived in fear of them my entire life, and had kept them safely at bay with my father's dream catcher. But with the dream catcher gone, perhaps, instead of running from them, I could see if I could glean any clues from them.

With a renewed determination, I climbed in bed and recalled a book I had once edited on lucid dreaming. There was a technique, MILD, it was called, though I forgot what it stood for, where one repeats an affirmation or mantra out loud as they fall asleep.

"I will discover who I am. I will discover who I am. I will discover who I am.." I repeated this hundreds of times before finally drifting off.

My tiny bare feet carry me down a hall. There is something in the room at the end I must get to. I reach the doorway and enter. He is there, on a stone slab. The old man. He is very wrinkled. His face is sunken. I go to his side, and place my tiny hand in his bony, emaciated fingers. His eyes go wide. He asks me something, and I whisper back. He smiles and breathes his last breath. He is gone. I climb on top and wail and cry. I do not want him to leave. I want him to come back. He is growing colder and stiffer, but I refuse to leave him. After a long time, someone is calling. Someone rushes in and picks me up. I scream and scream — I do not want to leave him, but I am being carried further away from him.

I woke up with tears streaming down my face, Paul and Stewie hovering over me with concern. Apparently they had been trying to wake me. I was breathing jaggedly, as if I'd been screaming and crying. Clearly I was acting out my dream. I closed my eyes and thought hard about it, trying to remember before it flitted away. I grabbed onto it and mentally combed through it as best as I could.

"My name! I told him my name!" I yelled. "The lost goddess in me — she is called Naoma!"

We all sat stunned for a moment.

"Naoma. It's beautiful, but I've never heard of the Goddess Naoma. Have you, Stewie?" Paul asked.

Stewie shook his head.

"Well, no time like the present to start researching," I said as I started climbing out of bed.

Stewie sighed. "I guess I'll make some coffee," He said as he headed for the door with me on his tail.

I was headed down to the computer in their office. Paul followed behind, as there was no point in sitting in an empty guest room.

---

6 hours later, and the research had turned up nothing. I had gone down every winding internet search path I could think of. Naoma was a Hebrew name that meant pleasant. I found a video game character who was a goddess with the name, but it seemed isolated and made up just for the video game.

I came across the Goddess Niobe, and she sounded

promising. Niobe was the epitome of a heartbroken mother who had lost all her children due to her own arrogance. That would certainly justify wanting to forget who you were, but that was laid to rest by Paul. He knew Niobe, and knew that she was still Upstairs, and so agoraphobic that she never left her home.

Naoma must be so forgotten that there was no record of her on Earth, at least one deciphered and discussed online. *Oh well.* At least I knew something. If only I knew who the old man in the dream was. He seemed so familiar, like it was on the tip of my tongue.

I walked into the kitchen. Paul was on the phone with someone. Whoever it was, he was clearly not enjoying the conversation.

"No. You'll get nothing from me," and he clicked the phone down.

"Gods not immune to telemarketers?" I kidded with him.

He gave me a weak smile. "Not exactly. That was your brother. Until your mother can be reached — we're still trying to reach her, just as you asked — he is considered your next of kin and the executor of your estate. He has your car, and was requesting I hand over anything of potential value you may have left at work, since your house was a total loss."

I went pale and sat down. I knew he was cruel, but it had only been about 48 hours since my supposed death, and here he was, picking over my belongings like a stranger, as if they had no blood bond at all.

His words from our dad's funeral came back to me. *Now I don't have to pretend you're my sister for a second longer.* Why would he say that, unless… "Paul, please drive me over to his shop. The ghost of Chuli has some cold hard truths to ask of him."

Paul gripped my hand as we walked in the shop. He knew the garage held many fond memories of my father, and he suspected, correctly, that seeing it again would be momentarily hard for me. But he also knew that I was made of strong stuff, and I would force myself to move past sentimentality quickly. I smiled at him, and let go of his hand.

Fortunately, Tolly was the only one working right now. Honestly, I wasn't even sure if the other mechanics, the ones that worked here for years, still worked here under my brother. Perhaps they didn't.

Tolly's legs were sticking out from underneath a car. The radio was on, so he didn't know we were here. I walked up to him and pulled his legs, rolling the cart he was laying on out from under the car in one swift movement.

"Hey! What the...aaah! Chuli!"

I watched in pleasure as the fear took hold and he lost all coloring.

"Why did you say I'm not your sister?"

Panicking, he squirmed away from me, jumped up, and tried to make for the door, but Paul blocked his path.

"You're supposed to be dead!" He whipped around, looking even more terrified now than he had before.

"Why, Tolly? I'm your sister! Why did you hate me so much? Why did you hurt me? Why? I loved you! And you treated me like garbage! Even now, you only see the value in my belongings."

It felt good to finally demand the answers to the questions I had always wanted answered. Tolly began to shake.

"Please, Chuli…I'm so sorry. Please don't send him after me again. Please, I'll do whatever you want."

Upon closer inspection, I noticed a series of bruises on Tolly. His face was still a bit puffy, and he had the remnants of two black eyes, and a crooked nose. Someone had beat the crap out of him, and I had a feeling I knew exactly who was responsible. A certain God who liked to punch first, ask questions later. Ram had mentioned he had ruled out my brother, but he hadn't mentioned that he'd potentially knocked him out as well.

Perhaps when I was younger, I would have felt obligated to feel bad about it, but the very last of my caring feelings for him had vanished this morning when he had shown zero remorse or sadness over my death. Even now, he was only apologizing out of fear for his own well being.

"What I want is answers! Why did you hate me? WHY?"

"Because I was jealous! Everything was great between me and Dad until you came along and ruined it! You with your little brown curls and big stupid brown eyes! Once you and your stupid flaky bitch of a mom came along...oww!"

Tolly flinched as I approached him and gripped his shirt in anger, pulling him upward, nearly off the ground.

"You leave my mother out of this!"

All the anger and frustration about the current situation was finding a wonderfully violent outlet in my brother. Perhaps there was something to be said for punching first and asking questions later.

"I'm sorry! Ow! OK! Let me go, please! I'm still sore from your boyfriend...aaah!"

Tolly cried out again as I let him go only to slap him, hard.

"He is not my boyfriend. He is just someone who recognizes a piece of shit when he sees one. We were a family, Tolly. I get that we don't have the same mother, but he was my Dad too. Of course he's going to love me!"

"But he's NOT your dad!" Tolly yelled. "He's MY dad! Don't you see? You were three years old when they met. You ran over to our site at a Pow-Wow. You told us your dad was an Indian too, just like him, but that he was far away. And I'll never forget the look on his face as you yammered on and on until your mom came to fetch you. He was totally absorbed and amused. He called you Chuli, and said you looked just like a little brown bird. And right at that moment, I knew. I fucking knew! Nothing would ever be the same again. He didn't give a shit about me, his actual son. All he cared about was you! Even when your mom left him, he still loved you — still kept you. Do you know what that felt like!? It fucking HURT, Chuli! And I vowed that you would hurt just as much as me, for taking my dad away from me."

Tolly stood there, drawing ragged breaths. I didn't know what to say as I stared at the face of my brother in my father's shop. Not my brother. Not my father. I turned away from him and walked to the door. Paul wrapped his arm around me, and we headed back to the Chateau.

———

sixteen

. . .

Chuli

IT HAD BEEN six full days since the fire and the frostbite. Six days since my life fell apart. Not even a week, yet it seemed nearly a lifetime. I was still at the Chateau, waiting for word from Ram, getting more anxious every day that went by without him.

To distract my thoughts from worry, I reflected on the long conversation I had over the phone with my mother yesterday. It was so good to hear her voice. She seemed totally at peace, like after all this time, she finally found the right place for her restless soul. After I explained everything that was happening to me — well, an abbreviated, god-free version — I finally worked up the courage to ask the tough questions I needed answers to. I really didn't want to talk about Tolly, so I went straight to the heart of the matter.

"Kunchen, who is my real father?"

My mother hesitated, but finally settled on an answer. "Your dad loved you, Chuli. Very much. You know that."

"I know that. But he wasn't my real father, was he? Chuli isn't even my real name. It's Naoma, isn't it?"

My visit with Tolly had given me some new insight into

my nightmare. There was a very long pause on the other end.

"You still there?"

"Yes, sweetie, I'm here. How do you know that?"

"I dreamt it. I'm right, aren't I?"

"You were named after your grandmother."

My mom had left home right out of high school and was estranged from her parents. I'd never met them, and only heard very limited stories about them when I pressed her as I got older. I assumed she didn't care for either of them, but apparently she had loved her mother enough to name her own daughter after her, at least originally.

"Who was my biological father? I have a right to know."

Another pause. *Maybe she had gotten very comfortable with silence during her vow.*

"His name was Arvind. We met when I was on a trip to India."

This time it was me who stayed silent as I waited for her to continue.

"We were happy together for a while, but as you got a little older, it became clear to me that he was reckless and irresponsible. I got scared, and I brought you back home to America. He promised he was going to do better, and from what I heard, he was trying. He was saving up to come to America to see us. And then..." her voice cracked with emotion, "...he was hit by a car and killed. I'm so sorry, Chuli, I should have told you all of this a long time ago. At the time, you were so little, I felt like it was OK to keep the truth from you. And then when you were older and so close with your dad, I figured it would only cause unnecessary pain."

There was another extended silence while I digested this information. Finally, I broke through the latest round of *Events That Turn Chuli's Life Upside Down, Phone Edition*. I was getting pretty good at expecting life-altering news these days.

"Something happened that got you scared, didn't it? Something with me. That's why we left." I thought about the old man that kept dying in my dream.

"Oh, Chuli…it was terrible." my mother cried. "You were gone for hours. Arvind was supposed to be watching you, but he lost you. We searched and searched, and finally found you. You were so sad and helpless, and screaming and crying in the dark on top of…"

"A dead man. I remember."

"You didn't stop crying for days. I was freaked out. I didn't know what to do, so I ran away with you. I wanted to get you as far away from that awful room with the man as I could." Her voice began to waver. "If I would have known we were never going to see your father again…" She let out a cry and began sobbing in earnest.

"Mom, I forgive you. It's OK. I would have wanted to try to shield my child from pain too."

We cried together, grieving a life that could have been. *Now I have two fathers to grieve.* After we calmed down, I promised I would try to get up to see her soon, just as soon as things here were settled.

After the phone call, I slept peacefully for a while. The nightmare with the old man had run its course, now that I knew the truth. Towards morning, however, the other, blurrier nightmare took shape once more. Pieces of it lingered, but it never told a full story.

A bitter taste. Yelling into an abyss. Someone shoving me. Falling, falling.

I woke up in the early dawn, gasping for breath. Now that I knew how Losts became...Lost, I believed I was dreaming of the last moments of the goddess inside me.

I snuck downstairs and made some tea. In the morning stillness and quiet, I contemplated all that I had just learned, and silently clicked all the pieces into shape. I was born in India. Sundar and Radha called me sister. Then I thought back to the first time I met Ram. He fainted at the sight of me. Fun-sucker was enthusiastically backing me up on this. *Holy shit,* I thought, as the pieces clicked together in my head. *Fun-sucker isn't my conscience. She's a Goddess! She has a real name: Revati.*

Ram was right. His wife hadn't committed suicide. She may have drunk the herbs and said the words, but the feeling of terror in my dream as she was shoved made me certain she hadn't wanted to jump. She wasn't even thinking about jumping. She was looking for something — someone. *She was looking for Ram.*

I closed my eyes and tried to directly connect to Revati, to call out to her inside my own head. Nothing. *How much of her remained trapped inside me? What happens to me if she breaks free? Would the Goddess consume me? Would I lose myself?*

I crept back up to my room, passing Stewie in the hallway. He gave me a soft and tired smile. He and Paul had been so kind to me, providing for my every need. I thought about what I could do to show my gratitude as I got dressed. At the moment, I was basically a homeless person with no identity and nothing to my name, so it wouldn't be anytime soon. *Someday, I thought, I'll make it up to them.* I put on one of the cute tops and jeans Stewie bought me. They fit perfectly. *Was fashion somehow another power that Stewie possessed?* I yearned to know more about him. Perhaps if I was lucky, he'd open up to me one day. For now, I'd settle with the obvious fact that he and Paul had a deep and devotional love, stronger than any couple I'd ever met, and he had Paul to confide in.

I descended the stairs, trying to push thoughts of my

new knowledge down so I didn't alarm Stewie. He was so very intuitive, I suspected he'd know something was up, and I wanted him to have at least one cup of coffee in his system before a round of *Morning Revelations with Chuli* began.

As I neared the bottom of the stairs, I froze. There was tapping on the kitchen door. I hid around the corner, hoping it was Ram, but prepared to stay hidden in case it was not.

"You're Stewie, right? Please...I had nowhere else to turn."

I recognized the voice. It was Zach! I had nearly completely forgotten about him in all that had happened.

He continued in an anguished voice. "She stopped responding to my texts. At first, I thought she was just mad at me, or got scared off or something. But I had this awful feeling, and..." Zach began to cry, "I heard from another author about the fire. I drove down here to see for myself. Please, please, tell me it's not true, that it's some kind of misunderstanding. She can't be gone!"

Zach cried some more. I didn't have deep feelings for him, but I still liked Zach as a person, and it was so hard to hear him in such pain. Pain that I could easily remedy, even if it was just to tell him we needed to break things off.

I didn't quite forget what Ram said about his hook-ups in the city. But I certainly didn't think poor Stewie, who had done so much for me already, should have to put up with a sobbing person in his kitchen first thing in the morning. Fun-sucker, *Revati,* I reminded myself, urged caution, but I forged on anyway, and rounded the corner before Stewie had even said a word.

"Chuli! Thank the gods!" Zach ran to me, relief flooding his face, and held me tight for a long time. He kissed my hair over and over again. I could feel him shaking.

"I'm okay, Zach. I'm here," I comforted him, before finally gently disentangling myself from his embrace.

He couldn't seem to stop himself from touching me, however. It was as if he needed to keep feeling me to make sure I wasn't a dream or a ghost. *Wow, I had no idea he cared this much.*

Unfortunately for him, I knew the feeling of needing to reach out and touch someone, but it was Ram's solid presence that I longed for.

"Chuli, what happened?" He said, settling on stroking my arm.

"Um, it's a long story, Zach, and I'd rather not get into it now."

Talking to Zach made me realize just how hard it was going to be to try to get any of my old life back at all. How would I explain the circumstances of my death/rebirth to every acquaintance I knew? Would anyone believe me, or would there always be some cloud of suspicion over me?

Zach was now petting my hair, and I resisted the urge to swat him away at this point. *Why had I come into the kitchen? This was a terrible idea.* Now that I elated him with news of my life, I had to deflate him with a "let's be friends" talk.

I took a deep breath and figured it was time to do some heartbreaking. I looked at Stewie, who was standing there in his kimono, frozen in place, watching the spectacle with an indecipherable look.

"Stewie, I think the coffee's ready. Why don't you get a cup? Zach and I need to talk. We'll be right out back on the patio. You'll be able to see me from the window. OK?"

Stewie looked skeptical, but also gave a longing look towards his percolator on the counter. He nodded and got a cup while I slipped my fuzzy new boots on and led the way to the patio behind the kitchen.

Outside was kind of nice. The snow had mostly melted, and there was a whisper of damp spring in the air. There was even a bird chirping somewhere. Two squirrels stopped chasing each other to watch them, then scurried off.

I parted my lips, trying to decide how to begin, but instantly, Zach was on me. He pulled me into a passionate embrace, and kissed me fiercely, shoving his tongue down my throat. I tensed and tried to pull away.

"Don't say it, don't you dare!" He pulled his lips just far enough away from mine to speak, then kissed me again.

It felt more like an assault at this point. I tried to turn my head, to get away, but he was strong and I was fully in his grip. I felt something sharp prick my side and a burning sensation.

"You will not be his again!" He held me closely pressed against him.

From the window, it would appear that we were hugging. Stewie wouldn't be able to see the panic on my face, and he was probably too far away from me to intuit the feelings of terror rolling through my body.

I felt the warmth of the Veruni Nectar rapidly spreading through my body from the place on my side. He must have injected me with it, and I realized, too late, that it was all an act. Zach had fooled us all. *What have I done?*

I fought with all my might, but the Veruni took hold. My mind stayed fighting, but my body reacted to his and came alive with fire. It embraced him back.

Once he was certain I was no longer going to fight him, he let go, and took my face in his hands. I closed my eyes. As long as I didn't look at him, I'd be OK.

"Open your eyes, love."

I refused, but he was clever. He began caressing my face, trailing kisses down my neck. My mind was horrified and screaming out, but there was no stopping my body's reaction to his kisses. My head fell back and my body melted into his.

He jumped on the opportunity and used his fingers to force my fluttering eyelids open while inches away from my face. Our eyes locked, and a powerful force slammed into my mind, nearly knocking me senseless.

He was beautiful. Absolutely perfect in every way. He was practically glowing. Anything else around him seemed to dim. *Oh, how I loved him. And oh, how I had hurt him!* My eyes pricked with tears.

"I'm so sorry I hurt you! Please, let me make it up to you," I said, while tenderly stroking his beautiful cheek.

He smiled back, and it filled my world with joy. "I know just the thing, Chuli. Follow me."

I blindly followed him down the path that led away from the house, without a single thought of doing otherwise.

Moments later, we arrived at the entrance to the old mine I had shown him on our hiking date. This time, some of the boards had been removed, creating a way in. He turned his phone flashlight on and led us in, just passed the boards, when he issued a command.

"Stay."

I froze in place. I would stay, because he had asked. I would not dare disobey. He went around and lit a series of lanterns, illuminating the room. In the shadows, I saw someone leaned against a plank, lying prone, but I was too far away to make out the details.

"Ok, you can come to me now."

I rushed forward, eager for an embrace from him. I wrapped myself around him, showering him with kisses.

"That's enough," he commanded as he pushed me away. My body stopped immediately and gave him space.

"Right now, I want to show you how you're going to make me very, very happy. Come see!"

I followed him to the man in the corner. As we got closer, I made out the prone man's features. It was Ram. He had been beaten very, very badly. His face was puffy, and dried blood was smeared all down the side of it, as if someone had hit him in the head. His arms and legs were bound with a series of ropes. Something deep inside of me screamed, but I had no outward feelings to show displeasure one way or another. Zach had promised me I could make him very happy, and I was eager to make it happen.

Zach spoke. "You don't remember, but this hunk of rotting meat," he kicked Ram for emphasis, eliciting a grunt," is your husband. But you're about to change that!"

I looked at Zach as he spoke. He was so animated! So strong. And so enthusiastic! *Why would I ever want to see that face sad?*

"How can I help?" I smiled at him.

He smiled back. "First, I want you to understand that this isn't just for me. It's not for you either, but honestly," He leaned into me conspiratorially, lowering his voice, "No one gives a shit about you."

He smiled again and backed up. "I'm going to tell you a story!"

I waited with rapt attention, eager to hear his beautiful voice tell the tale.

"Once upon a time, there lived a beautiful princess named Revati. That was you. Your father, King Kakudmi, thought you were the fairest in the land. He was right, too. You were so sweet and full of beauty, grace, and humility. Not nearly as cocky and self-assured as you are now."

I felt the burn of shame as this beautiful man judged me and found me lacking.

"In childhood, as was the way back then, you were promised to a powerful prince from a different kingdom, far away. That prince was me, Zahhak. I was handsome and clever — a perfect match for you. But tragedy intervened. After an accident left my father dead, your stupid father decided I was no longer fit to be your husband, and he took you away! I tried to follow to take you back. NO ONE STEALS FROM ME!"

He yelled out, the anger still palpable. "I even found a way to become a god myself, but by the time I found you again, it was too late. He had married you off to this buffoon right here," He kicked Ram again, who seemed to be slowly coming to.

"Chuli…fiii..." He rasped out.

I looked at him. Something stirred inside me again. *Pain. Terror.* I felt Zach's powerful arm on my shoulder.

"Don't look at him. I'm the only one here you care about."

I looked at him and teared up. "I'm so sorry — you're right. Please continue."

I continued to stare at him in awe, but deep inside, I could feel the separate entity of anger and terror growing.

"So, as I was saying before I was so RUDELY..." and he kicked Ram in the side, causing another grunt, "...interrupted, was that you had already been married when I found you again. I had to find a way to get you back — I ALWAYS get what's mine! I worked my way into your royal court with my knowledge of herbs and magic, and became your official healer. As I watched you over the years, it caused me anguish to see how you cared about him. He would galavant around, cocky and self-assured, leaving you for days at a time to go slay demons without a care for how you worried for him, how you missed him when he wasn't there. You were so loyal, so caring. You never would have left his side. But you were supposed to be MINE! You were supposed to worry over ME, Revati!"

I backed up a bit, so sorry, so sad for him. "I'm so sor.."

He cut me off. "First, I thought if he was gone long enough, you might forget your love for him, so I drugged him up good at the Yamuna. But after months with him distracted in the river, you grew more and more distraught instead, convinced that something was amiss. I tried to tell you he didn't care, but then you turned on me! You told me I didn't know anything about what it felt like to have your love taken from you."

Zach was growing angrier and more desperate. He got closer to me again. "But I did know! I knew all too well! So that's when I knew. I had to kill the Revati that was. I had to make her forget. And it worked!"

I stood, enraptured at the tale, while the anger warred inside me. He drugged Ram. He killed Revati. He ruined their lives, all because her father had broken a promise, probably with good reason. *But he was so beautiful. He must know what is right for me! He must know what is good!*

"How did you find me again?" I wondered.

He smiled, pleased with himself. I was glad to make him feel good, and it made me smile too.

"That's one of my special powers. Finding people. That, and charm," he smiled a very dashing smile and I felt myself melt from its prettiness. "Once I built enough followers on Earth with my early blog posts about Druid herbs, my powers began to grow. But oh, sweet irony of ironies, that as I signed my book deal with Burning Wind Press, that you should happen to be the editor. I couldn't believe my good fortune!" He laughed, and I laughed too.

"When I was certain you didn't remember me or anything about Revati's past, I thought it was a great new beginning, and it was a chance to have you love me in earnest, built the old fashioned way. Such a novel idea! I had waited for so long to get you back, I thought it couldn't hurt to wait a little more. I decided to seal the deal with Veruni on New Years, because when it comes down to it, I don't actually give a flying fuck what your true feelings are for me." He laughed.

I smiled and nodded in understanding. My body

wanted to lash out, but I was still frozen into obedience by the Veruni. My emotions were tied to his emotions.

"But then that stupid traffic jam made me late, and that stupid girl had wasted the Veruni on you. She paid for it later, of course. I was glad to see you hadn't accidentally been tied to another with it, but tell me, what DID happen to you that night?"

I was still unable to look at Ram since Zach's previous command not to, so I pointed in his direction instead. "He kept me blindfolded until it passed."

"Oh, noble Ram! Fucking up YET AGAIN! You had a chance to tie her to you for good, and you wasted it! Oh, this is rich." He laughed again and I laughed too. "What are the odds that this wife stealer would end up finding you again? At this moment! And YOU..." He grabbed me by the hair, "YOU had the nerve to attempt to choose him over me! AGAIN!"

I cried out in pain and shame. "I'm so sorry. Please...let me make it up to you. I didn't know!"

He relaxed his grip and calmed himself. He smiled a cool smile. "The marriage of Ram and Revati was linked by magic in the wedding ceremony Upstairs. Now, you will make it up to me. You will magically unlink it. You are about to get divorced, so you can marry me, the way it was always meant to be. Now, drink some of this."

Zach picked up a cup sitting on a ledge nearby and handed it to me. It smelled foul, but I dared not upset him. I forced two sips down before retching.

"Give the rest to him," he said, pointing at Ram.

I took the cup and approached him, placing it near his lips.

"Chuli, Revati, please, don't do this..."

The words caused pain to sear my insides, but I held the cup to his lips and poured it in. He choked and gasped, and I forced more down his throat again.

"Please, you are strong. Fight him. Save us." Ram's words were whispered only loud enough for me to hear.

"OK, that's enough. Let's not drown him before we can complete the ceremony." Zach chuckled, and approached me with a dagger. It was a beautiful ornate silver thing, clearly used in rituals. "Now, take this, and draw blood, in a small x just above his heart."

Zach took Ram's thin tunic and ripped it open further at the neckline, revealing his chest. I took the knife, and did as I was told. Ram flinched. I was still trapped by Zach's words, but fighting...fighting for the surface.

"Good! Hey...cheer up," as I stood upright again, he took my sad, downcast face and turned it towards his, kissing me gently. All thoughts of anger vanished. *Oh, sweet kiss of love! Zach loved me!* I was the luckiest woman alive.

He took my hands, which still held the bloodied dagger, and held them towards my chest. He delicately unbuttoned my top until it was open enough to reveal the expanse of skin above my heart. The movements made my breath ragged with desire.

"Now cut yourself, love." I watched the lust in his eyes grow as I maimed myself, slicing an x to match the one on Ram's chest.

He wanted me. I would hurt myself a million times if it brought him pleasure.

"Now, look Ram in the eyes, and tell him you release him of his duties as husband. Mingle your blood with his."

I rubbed my finger on the blood growing from my chest and went to Ram. I leaned down, and placed my bloodied finger upon the wound in his chest. I looked him in the eyes as best I could, but it was difficult because of the swelling. He looked so broken, all the way through.

Sadness mixed with anger began seeping through me again as I spoke. "I…release you from your duties as my husband."

I felt a strange surge go through me. Ram bucked as well, as if he had felt the same. I turned to Zach. He smiled, and I smiled back.

"And now Ram's part is finished here. Time to send this sad sack on his way."

He took the dagger from me, and was just about to slice through Ram's neck when I stopped him.

"Wait!"

He turned to me, with a cold, displeased glare.

"I...let me do it. If he ruined our life together and caused you pain, it would be my honor to send him away," I gently touched his beautiful cheek in wonder.

He smiled again, and so did I. Zach handed me the dagger and stood close by my side as I hovered over a very resigned looking Ram.

"Don't send me away, please...Naoma," Ram whispered again. An image flashed before me: The old man in my dream, face sunken, lying on the slab. The smile as I told him my name — the bereftness I felt as he departed his body. *Ram. He came back for me.*

I gripped the dagger, and with all the strength inside me, jabbed it as hard as I could into the side of his neck.

---

seventeen

• • •

Chuli

EVERY LAST BIT of my heart and soul dissolved into anguish as I watched the life seep out of the man before me. I sobbed and cried out and fell to my knees in front of where he lay, pulling at my hair. *It was my fault. I had killed him. Why!?*

I took in the ghastly wound, the handle still jutting out of his beautiful neck. I grabbed it and gently pulled it out, turning it towards myself. I looked at him one more time before I was going to end my own miserable, worthless life as punishment.

He wore a look of shock and surprise as blood poured out of the wound, draining his face of all color. He took one last raspy breath, blood trickling out of the corner of his mouth, and died.

I leaned forward, wretched, and vomited. As the wave of nausea receded, so too did the Veruni nectar, and my head cleared.

I was free.

I took a few steadying breaths, staring at my shaky hand that still held the dagger. I dropped it and it fell into the puddle of blood that had pooled next to Zach's body.

I jumped to my feet as concern over Ram flooded back in and I frantically began removing the ropes binding his arms.

"Chuli..." No words followed, but no words were needed.

I had done it. I had saved us both.

Flashlight beams penetrated the mine, and we heard voices calling my name.

"Here! We're in here!" I turned and yelled, ending the moment.

Stewie and Paul rushed forth. They paused and took in the gruesome scene. I was a bloodied, smeared mess. On the floor lay a very dead Zach in a pool of blood and vomit. And angled next to me on the plank was a very bloodied, tortured Ram, who seemed to be slipping back out of consciousness and desperately in need of medical attention.

"Help him," I croaked, pointing to Ram.

Paul wrapped me in his comforting arms. A man I didn't know — he must've arrived with Paul & Stewie — procured a bottle from his pocket and began pouring something down Ram's throat as he gasped and sputtered. Idun's Extract. He was going to be OK.

"Hey! You from the High Order?" I yelled at the man.

He looked up. In the dark, he looked very menacing, but I was too numb to be intimidated at the moment. He gave a slight nod.

I gestured towards Zach's body. "You caught him Upstairs?"

He nodded again. "His name is Zahhak. May he burn in Hell, if it's real."

The man stared at me, but it was impossible to decipher the look on his face in the dark. I turned and exited the mine with Paul and Stewie on my heels.

The morning daylight hurt my eyes for a moment. Once

I adjusted, I looked around the forest of Bear Mountain and found what I sought.

I saw a deer waiting in the shadows, and knew that she had led my friends to my location. I nodded a thank you, hands clasped together in prayer, then numbly tread the path back down to the Chateau.

———

eighteen

. . .

Chuli

WE SAT ON THE SOFA. I leaned against Paul, with a very shaken Stewie leaning on him on the other side. He was pumping out so much calming energy I wondered if he was going to pass out soon from the effort.

I had assured Stewie that I was the only one to blame for my actions that morning, and he was not to feel guilty, but he still hadn't said a word or lost the haunted look on his face. I was still too numb to offer any further comfort, and I wasn't sure if he would've taken it anyway.

I had scrubbed myself beyond clean in the shower, my new outfit tossed in the trash. It had too much blood to even consider saving. I took some gauze and tape I had found in the bathroom and covered the nasty cut on my chest. It probably needed stitches, but I figured a doctor's office or hospital was off limits, and I didn't have any magical elixirs of my own. As long as I kept it clean, I figured it would be fine eventually. It would leave an ugly scar, but it would only match the scar that was sure to form on the inside as well.

I looked at my hands as we sat. I could still feel the way the dagger felt in my hand, the resistance it encountered when it punctured the skin of Zach's neck. It was nothing like the little pen knife I had used on Tolly, the one that had lived in my pocket up until my belongings were stolen and burned. My hand began to shake.

I jumped up and headed to the kitchen. "I'm making tea. Anyone want a drink?"

I got no response. I went to the kitchen, wanting to give the two of them some more private time to talk. I turned the kettle on, and washed a few mugs in the sink to keep my hands busy. I wondered how, and where, Ram was. I needed to make a decision about what to do with my future, although since it was still only afternoon, I half joked to myself that this day was never going to end, so I probably didn't have to plan anything.

Honestly, I had no idea how I was going to move forward here in town after what happened. Probably the High Order would keep the situation at the mine hidden from the police, but how did I go about coming back from the dead?

There was a knock on the kitchen door. Instinctively, I grabbed a knife from the magnet strip to defend myself as Paul entered the kitchen. He looked at me and took in the knife I was gripping, but didn't say anything. He went to the door and opened it. It was the man who'd saved Ram.

He stared at me with a calculating gaze, ignoring Paul's glare at the way he stepped right in before being invited. I thought of Paul's sanctimonious bastards comment earlier regarding the High Order. That description seemed appropriate, but since he had saved Ram's life, I wasn't going to judge him too harshly.

He was tall, thick and muscular, with a shaved head, and full military fatigues. He looked as if he could snap me like a twig before I could manage a single lunge with the knife. I dropped it, and it clanged onto the counter.

"Chuli Davis?" He spoke with a gravelly voice, the kind soldiers followed into battle.

He must be some kind of war god. I stared at him. It seemed too obvious a question to even answer.

Paul kissed me on the cheek on his way back to the living room. "I'll be right in the other room if you need me," and he strolled away.

"I understand you have suffered significant losses during this affair."

Still I just stood there. Once again, it was too obvious to warrant an answer.

"Most of your losses were due to the criminal actions of the perpetrator. However, it is our understanding that our officer on the ground failed to take adequate measures to protect you."

I jumped to Ram's defense. "It wasn't his fault! He didn't do anything wrong. He protected me — he saved my life!"

He continued to stare, my words having zero effect on his countenance. "He eliminated the perpetrator from the list of suspects, thereby allowing him to commit further crimes, including the death of a human woman, the drugging of two others, the destruction of your personal property and human persona, the near hypothermic death of your mortal shell, and your ultimate capture by allowing you to remain in an unsecured location."

He listed these items as if he were reading formal charges against Ram. "Furthermore, he used his own extract to save you, thereby committing a crime against the High Order code. He will be punished accordingly."

"Zach was beyond clever. He was a master at hiding the truth. Surely you don't place the blame solely on Ram? He is a damn fine agent! If anything, it's my own fault! Zach was right in front of me the whole time, and I never saw it coming. I willingly left the protection of this house to be with him. Blame me!"

As I talked, I walked closer, until I laid my arm on his forearm. It was as solid as granite. Some kind of weird power zapped up through my arm, but I didn't flinch. Helping Ram was my priority right now, and I didn't want anything to distract from my words.

The agent, who apparently didn't have a name or wasn't willing to divulge it to me, stared at where I touched him and then back at my face, looking entirely unmoved. I removed my hand. He set a briefcase he'd been carrying down on the counter and opened it, placing a series of documents in front of me. One was a birth certificate, written in both English and another language I assumed was Hindi.

Naoma Devi Bhatt.

Mother: Linda Ann Richards.

Father: Arvind Bhatt.

Another was a passport — an Indian passport. Behind that was a shiny, driver's license looking card, the picture from my old driver's license smiled back at me. It was a green card, giving me, Naoma Devi Bhatt, permanent resident status in the United States. I stared in awe and wanted to cry, but swallowed hard and blinked rapidly to halt my emotions in front of the war god or whatever he was.

"Chuli Davis is deceased. You are Ms. Bhatt. This packet of information includes instructions on how to access your bank account. The account contains US $500,000. That should be sufficient to see you re-homed out of state and to buy an assortment of material goods."

He placed a set of keys on the table next to the documents.

"Here are keys to the safehouse. I believe you are

familiar with it. The former agent on your case will have his belongings removed and it will be ready for your use by approximately 9:00 am tomorrow. You may stay there for up to 48 hours while you make permanent accommodations. In exchange, you will be silent on this matter. You will tell no one what happened. You will move out of state, at least 100 miles away, and not visit this place again or contact anyone that resides here. Can we count on your discretion?"

He held his large, callused hand out, seeking a handshake to seal the agreement.

"What would happen if I said no?" I was already planning on agreeing. *What was the use of telling the local police anyway? They wouldn't believe me.* No one would, but I thought it was important to know my options.

"That is not a recommended course of action," he said, his hand dropping down to momentarily rest on the handle of some sort of pistol strapped to his thigh. I shuddered, and held out my hand to shake.

He took my hand in his. His grip was firm, but he refrained himself from crushing the bones in my hand, a feat I was certain he could accomplish. I winced as the up-and-down movement of the shake caused the cut on my chest to rub against its bandage.

"You are injured," he stated, while staring at the area where the outline of the bandage left a lump under my shirt. I looked down at it as well, and saw that blood was starting to seep through. Maybe stitches were a good idea after all.

He returned his gaze to my face.

"May I treat it?"

"Is that a High Order approved activity?" I snarked.

Paul's pessimism towards the "sanctimonious bastards" was beginning to rub off on me, especially after I had just been so casually threatened with death. The agent just continued to look at me, waiting for my consent. I nodded, because honestly, it would be foolish to refuse treatment from someone who probably had access to an assortment of magical elixirs.

I sat down in a chair at the kitchen table and unbuttoned my shirt enough to expose the wound. After washing his hands at the sink, The agent kneeled down on the floor next to me, laying a medical kit on a nearby chair. With a gentleness I didn't think possible from someone with such strength, he removed the bandage and investigated the cuts.

I closed my eyes, trying to block out the pain and the uncomfortableness of having a stranger so near to me. I heard him unzip his medical bag and begin to remove supplies.

"I'm using dissolvable stitches," he said in a near whisper, since he was so close to me. He smelled like..rocks? The desert? I wasn't sure. *Probably somewhere with lots of death.*

I opened my eyes again and watched as he began to thread a curved needle. I noted that from this angle, I could see the top of his head, and the shadow of a full head of hair if he didn't shave it. To distract myself from the pain, I wondered at this. I had always assumed men shaved their heads when their hair was thinning, or they were bald on top, or some other reason.

It stung as the needle went in and the skin was tugged. I closed my eyes again, and tried to concentrate on taking deep breaths, in and out, as he worked, but that moved my chest too much, so I had to lower the focus to breathing from my diaphragm.

I heard the clink of the needle being returned to the chair, and he deftly tied off the end somehow. I watched him as he took some kind of cream in a tin, put a little to his finger, and slowly and with a feather-light touch, applied it to the cut. It felt warm and tingly in a good way, and the pain receded quickly. *Gods bless these High Order drugs,* I thought, as I took a deep breath, able to breathe much easier now.

"Better?" He asked.

He had tucked away his kit before I got a chance to see what the magical cream was, and he was now washing his hands at the sink again. He was turned away from me, so he didn't see me nod, forcing me to speak.

"Much, thank you."

He nodded in acknowledgement, then left without saying anything else. I don't know what else he would have said at that point anyway. It struck me as a strange way to leave, but nothing was normal about any of this.

After the agent was gone, Paul and Stewie came into the kitchen. They had been eavesdropping on the conversation, so I didn't have to fill them in on anything. They seemed a little concerned that I hadn't told them the extent of my injury and asked for their help with it, and I tried my best to smooth it over by changing the subject to the paperwork in front of me.

After we combed over the document packet together, Paul spoke.

"Ms. Bhatt," Paul pronounced formally, "There happens to be a vacant position at my publishing press. The chief shareholders," he gestured to Stewie, "and I would be honored to hire you as Editor in Chief. Naturally, as you are a very private person, we will respect your wishes and keep your image off any printed or virtual publication. We are currently closed during this time of great transition, as we move our offices to New York City. However, we'd be happy to assist you with moving and transition to city life."

I teared up, beyond grateful to my friends. Throwing myself back into work was just the routine I needed to figure out how to go forward in life, and they knew it.

I hugged them both as I cried. "I love you both so much. I don't know how to thank you."

I had just lost my life as Chuli Davis, but my life as Naoma Bhatt was just beginning.

I went upstairs and changed into my last clean shirt and admired the agent's handiwork in the mirror. My cut was now a very neat X, tied together with tight, perfectly even stitches, and was already healed past the bleeding stage, as if I had taken perfect care of the stitches for days.

I poured peroxide on the blood stain of my shirt and put it in the laundry, hoping it wasn't ruined. I was already down one of the three outfits I owned, and I wouldn't able to shop for anything else until I was at least 100 miles from here.

I came back down to the kitchen, where Stewie got to work preparing another glorious meal of Ram's produce for a late lunch. He seemed to be coming around a little. I wondered if the greenhouse would be cleaned out, or if the garden would be waiting for me tomorrow. I tried my hardest to keep my feelings about Ram at bay.

As we were eating, Stewie watched me closely. "You don't have to stay there, you know. You can stay with us."

Of course he could feel my apprehensions about moving into Ram's place, and how empty it would feel with him gone.

Paul had been right to warn me about getting my heart involved. Ram was leaving by morning, and he never even came to say goodbye. Perhaps he was too heartbroken. I tried to smile, and assured Stewie I would be fine there. I had been third-wheeling their relationship way too much lately, and wanted to give them a break from me and all my drama, even if it was only for a few days until we stayed together at their place in the city.

If I could live through this past week, I can handle a little heartbreak, I assured myself to help ease the pain in my chest. If only I could see him one last time, to ensure he was OK after this morning's events. The resigned look on his swollen, bloodied face as he thought I was going to kill him kept flashing into my mind, unbidden. I had been through a lot, but Ram could be utterly destroyed inside. I wished I knew how to help him.

Stewie got up from the counter and went to the key rack by the door. He handed me the keys to their car.

"Go. Get some closure." Of course he knew.

I hugged him again, then threw on my boots. They were still speckled with blood, but they would have to do. I had a god to catch.

---

nineteen

. . .

Chuli

THE SUN WAS low in the sky as I pulled up to the house. Ram's car was nowhere in sight. *Was he already gone?* I got out and knocked on the door, my heart hammering with nerves the longer I waited. I was just about to give up when the door opened.

Ram stood in the doorway and I swept my eyes over him, looking for confirmation that he was alive and well. He seemed to be. He backed up, allowing me to come inside.

"I'm sorry I'm still here. I heard you'll be staying here, so I was trying to get the place cleaned up and ready for you. I can leave right now, if you'd prefer."

"Why would I want you to leave? I came here hoping to find you." As usual, I was mystified by his behavior.

"Oh. ok, go ahead then." He walked over and sat down on the sofa.

I sat next to him. Ram looked me in the face. His eyes and face were no longer puffy, but there were still mottled bruises, especially creeping towards his hairline where he had been hit with something.

I longed to reach out and gently touch the lump there. I wished I could take all the pain away from him. Despite the rapid healing, he still looked so broken.

"Go ahead and what?"

"Yell at me. Hit me. Scream at me. Tell me you hate me, that I'm the worst High Order officer to walk the Earth. That I'm the worst husband to ever walk the Upstairs." He paused, his voice cracking. "I failed you, Chuli. I failed you, and I failed Revati. And I was such a coward, I didn't even have the guts to tell you the truth about who you were. I was afraid you'd..." He cut himself off and looked down again, and wiped some tears away.

"Afraid I'd what?" I reached out to touch his face. He gently took my hand to stop me, but couldn't quite let go of it, so he wound up holding it in his lap.

"I was afraid I'd lose you too, Chuli. That you would think I only cared because Revati's soul remains trapped inside of you. But the truth is...more complicated than that."

I could only imagine what it must feel like to find yourself attracted to the woman who magically divorced you from your dead wife who resides trapped inside her. *Complicated sounds about right.* He was still holding my hand.

"I didn't come here to do any of those things, Ram. I just wanted to make sure you were OK. The last time I saw you, you were so badly mangled. It was awful." I forced myself to swallow down the lump forming in my own throat. "What happened to you?"

"I reported back to the High Order, and ensured certain safety measures were put into place to protect you. Then I went to the gym to talk to the employees, to see if I could glean anything from them, or maybe follow them. Zach must have told them to be on the lookout for me, because I didn't even get two steps inside the door before someone snuck up from behind and whacked me over the head with something. The next thing I remember is waking up to see you, smiling at Zach. It took me a moment to clear my head enough to comprehend that what was happening was real, and not some nightmare."

He tried to collect his composure again and distracted himself by looking down at his arms. "I'm not sure what happened to me between the gym and the mine. I must've been beaten multiple times. I've had twice the normal dosage of Idun's, and I'm still sore. It's no more than I deserved though." He looked as if he was disappointed that he had survived. "So now that you know I'm OK, I should probably go. The High Order would have a fit if they knew I was talking to you right now. I am officially suspended." He set my hand down and stood up.

"Ram, wait." I stood up too, and stood in front of him, staring at his chest. Quietly, I whispered, "Can I see it?"

After a moment, Ram acquiesced. He opened the buttons on his shirt, revealing an ugly pink scar in the shape of an X above his heart. I gingerly touched it with my fingers.

"I'm so sorry," I whispered, not bothering to try to stop the tears flowing down my face.

"I am too," he whispered back. He too, shed tears. "Can you feel her inside you? Do you remember anything of our life together?" He placed his forehead against mine.

"Sort of. I get certain feelings, dreams sometimes, but I can't talk to her."

Ram was crying in earnest now. "I got there right after it happened. I had finally broken free from the Veruni, and got home. Someone at the palace told me she had headed to the bluffs with the healer. I remember him now. He was standing near the edge. I was calling for her. He was the one that told me she had jumped. He said he had tried to stop her, but she insisted that death was better than being married to a husband as awful as me. I didn't want to believe it. I jumped down to Earth, determined to find her, so sure I could make it right. I still wanted to find her, to apologize. To make it up to her somehow. To have her leave like that, it destroyed me. She didn't want to be with me. She chose death."

"But she didn't," I cut him off. " I dreamt of her death, Ram. She didn't want to kill herself at all. She was worried about you, looking for you. Zach tricked her into drinking the herbs and saying the incantations before he pushed her. Maybe he told her it was a locating spell. He admitted as much, remember? He wasn't lying. She loved you."

"Wh.." He started to talk, then stoped. Sometimes there weren't words to say. He clung to me in a tight hug and cried. We stayed like that for a while until he composed himself enough to continue.

"As the years and centuries went by with no trace of her, his words weighed heavier and heavier on my soul. I had finally given up and resolved to die. First my mortal shell, and then, when I returned Upstairs, I was planning on following her path. I wanted to die. To forget. To be Lost. But just before my last breaths on Earth, I turned my head, and..." He pulled us apart enough to look closely at me, his hands cradling the sides of my face. "There you were, with your big brown eyes and your curly hair, smiling at me, holding my hand. Somehow, you had found me."

"I remember. I told you my name."

"Naoma. Yes. I was so happy. You knew me, and I knew where you were! So when I reached the portal, I put in a request to have my own name and a similar form, to help you remember. When I got my knowledge, I joined the High Order so I could have access to their network, and I built a database in my search for you. I was so close to tracking you down. I had your first name, Naoma. But then, I got pulled away, to come to America to work on a drug case. I was annoyed, but what could I do? You can't argue with the High Order. You go where they send you. So I came here."

"And you found me. And...fainted." I smiled through my tears.

He smiled too. "I did. I was so shocked and confused, I actually fainted. I had spent eons searching for you, but it turns out, I had spent no time at all thinking about what I should say, exactly. You knew me as the child Naoma, but as the woman Chuli, you did not. I hadn't anticipated that, so I waited. And watched. And then you got drugged, so I had to do something. But the longer it went on, the harder it became to tell you."

"I have a confession. Remember when I was so mad at you for tracking my phone and crashing my date?"

He nodded slightly, our foreheads touching again. Somehow whispering, heads together like this, made it easier for the words to form.

"Well, the reason I was mad at you wasn't because of my phone. I had a...dream about you, and it kept popping into my head, unbidden, in the days following. It was very frustrating. But now, I'm wondering if it was maybe a real memory of you. A memory that is so strong with Revati that it somehow penetrated the surface."

"Tell me," Ram whispered.

"We were in a town, or a city. There was a monster, and I watched you slay it from above. You were magnificent and shimmering, and covered in gold jewelry. I began to climb down to greet you and cheer for you like so many others were, and then you were there. And you only had eyes for me. You helped me down and picked me up, and carried me inside a house,"

The energy around us began to take on a different feel.

"That," Ram whispered, his mouth creeping closer to mine, "was very real. And very, very, memorable. We were newly married. She was the most beautiful thing I had ever seen. And the way she looked at me..." he said, his lips creeping closer still.

Our breaths both became jagged with desire. "That is how she wants to remember you. I feel certain. And so do I," and with that, I closed the gap, pressing our lips together. It was like putting a flame to kindling. Our kisses became frantic, as if they were made of oxygen, and the only way we could breathe. I finished unbuttoning his shirt and pulled it off his arms. He grunted with a bit of pain, so I began kissing every bruise I saw. I kissed his scar too, wanting to kiss every last inch of him. He pulled my shirt up over my head as I worked. I wasn't wearing a bra, and he backed up to get a better view of me.

"Gods help me. You're exquisite," he exclaimed, before claiming my lips once more. I opened to him and deepened the kiss.

"The bed," I panted between kisses. We started working our way towards the bedroom, stopping here and there on the way to shed the rest of our clothing. By the time we fell onto the mattress, we were both naked. We explored each other's bodies, driving each other to new heights of desire, until I could take no more.

"Ram, I need…" I whimpered. He was kissing my breast, his hand traveling down towards my core. I cried out as he reached it, skilled fingers working their magic.

I opened my legs wide for him. "Ram, please..."

My hand traveled down as well, to stroke him and give him the kind of pleasure I was receiving. He groaned in response. He was now braced on his forearms over me and he kissed me again, bringing his hard length down closer to my entrance. I bucked upward, eager for the union. And then, with one swift motion, he was in me, filling me completely. I cried out in pleasure.

As we began to rock together in motion, I was creeping closer, closer, to the edge of a precipice. I cried out with animalistic noises, feral with desire. I forgot who I was as I connected with the divine force of Kundalini Energy.

"Oh, gods, Chuli..." Ram grunted.

Our pace quickened, Ram slamming harder and harder into me. I met him each time, gripping him as tight as I could. I was so close now. The shuddering broke through my final barrier, and I exploded into the universe, a million distant glittery pieces of gold. Ram cried out with one final explosion, deep inside me.

Afterward, we lay together for several long moments to catch our breath, arms entwined. I was staring at him, touching him. He was so beautiful. His bruises seemed to be fading, but there were still traces of them in the dim light. Once again, I was struck with a powerful urge to offer him comfort, to take his pain away. I started with one of the angrier bruises on his shoulder. I traced it with my finger, as if I was somehow luring the pain to the surface. I placed a delicate kiss there, visualizing the pain vanishing. Ram lay still, enraptured by my movements, allowing me full access to the myriad bruises and cuts.

When I was certain I had kissed each one on his body, I pulled myself up to face him, and began to do the same to his face, and finally the lump on his head. Then, I turned to his closed eyelids and kissed them too, before turning to his lips.

"Let me take your pain away," I whispered.

I kissed him sweetly, with love and care, as if he were made of precious glass. He responded in kind. We made love again, this time slowly, delicately, entwining our hearts. As we lay in the dark together, breathing peacefully, I thought about the complicated situation we were in, and how to make this work. We'd have to have a talk about what's next, but for tonight, everything was perfect and I didn't want to ruin this beautiful moment. It could wait until morning.

As I was drifting off, I heard him whisper, "You will be with me always, my love. Both of you."

---

twenty

. . .

Chuli

I SLEPT sounder than I had in months, maybe even years. I awoke to birds singing in the distance, and sunlight beaming into the room. I'd been having a lovely dream, but now it flitted away, leaving no real trace as to what it was about. I was so comfortable. For a moment, I forgot where I was as I stretched.

I was naked. In Ram's bed. My bed. I sat up and looked around. There was no sign of him. I looked over on the nightstand to see what time it was. 9:30. Something small and metal caught my eye next to the clock, and I picked it up to examine it. It was Ram's ring, the one he always wore. *His wedding ring*. I silently caressed it, then set it down again. I climbed out of bed, wrapping myself in the comforter from the bed. It smelled like him — like us.

As I wandered through the house, I swore I heard a woman crying somewhere. I tried to follow where the sound came from, but it never seemed to grow any louder or any softer. I decided to call out. "Hello? You OK?"

The crying stopped.

"Hello?" The same voice that had been crying called out. "Can you hear me?"

"Yes, just tell me where you are, and I'll find you!"

My adrenaline began pumping, so I paced back and forth, waiting for further direction.

"You can't come find me, Chuli, you stupid...husband stealer! I'm inside you!"

The voice cried out in a heavy accent. An Indian accent. And then it began wailing in earnest. I froze. I took a deep breath, closed my eyes, and opened them again. Tentatively, I finally spoke.

"Revati?"

---

dual: book 2

. . .

WAIT, that's it?!

Yep. Sorry! But fear not! That's only the beginning! **Sararuch.com** has more information for you, including bonus materials about characters, and how to get your hands on book 2, Dual! Here is a preview:

> Naoma Bhatt is trying her best to move forward with her new life, despite a number of major set-backs this past year, including losing both her entire past identity and her previous version of reality as she knew it. When two gods overdose on a mysterious and deadly venom at the biggest event of the decade, she's offered an opportunity to turn the tables and play the hero instead of the victim this time. Does she have what it takes to see the mission through, despite the voice in her head?
>
> Thank you for reading!

---

about the author

Sara Ruch's tarot cards used to tell her she should stop living in a fantasy world. She didn't listen. Instead, she writes about the worlds she creates, sometimes fictional, sometimes not. She lives in the mountains of Pennsylvania with her loving and supportive family and friends, a few furry & feathered creatures, and all the flora and fauna a woman could ask for.

Learn more at sararuch.com

acknowledgments

I have had so much encouragement, love, and support from my friends & family for this little dream of mine that I could just burst at the seems with gratefulness. I love you all!

Kyle O'Brien, I appreciate you wasting your valuable time copy editing back when I was a flighty POV flipflopper. You rule, my clueless compatriot!

Amanda Bombico, your keen editorial observations and suggestions helped me tremendously. Thank you!

Thank you especially to my husband Kevin, for your unwavering faith that I can do this, and to my incredible kids, who literally **published a print copy of this book on their own** for me, just to prove it was worthy. It will always be my most cherished copy.

Finally, I would like to acknowledge and thank YOU, dear reader, for getting this far! I hope you enjoyed this first leg of your journey Upstairs. If you know someone who might enjoy the ride as well, please share it with them. Thank you!

Made in United States
North Haven, CT
28 October 2022

26036145R00118